Burned

Julie Herman

Burned

Copyright © 2017 by Julie Herman

All rights reserved. No part of this book may be reproduced or transmitted in any form or by any means without written permission of the author.

ISBN 978-0-9974575-3-7

PONY CLUB is a trademark of The United States Pony Clubs, Inc., used with permission. For permissions or to learn more about the Pony Club experience visit ponyclub.org.

Oconee Spirit Press, Waverly, TN www.oconeespirit.com

Library of Congress Cataloging-in-Publication Data

Herman, Julie.

Burned/ Julie Herman

1. Teenage girls - Juvenile fiction. 2. Horses—Juvenile fiction. 3. Young adult fiction. 4. Horses—Fiction.

10 9 8 7 6 5 4 3 2 1

Printed and bound in the United States. The text paper is SFI certified. The Sustainable Forestry Initiative® program promotes sustainable forest management.

Illustrations © Jessica Mattea Dupree

Cover Image © Sushytskyi Serhii | Dreamstime.com

Cover Image © Yurii Bohdanov | Dreamstime.com

Cover design by Dead Center Graphics

Dedicated

to my fellow Chief Horse Management Judges at the United States Pony Clubs. We have the best job ever—playing with the kids in the barns.

Acknowledgments

I am so grateful for the wonderful early reads from the following writers: Martha, Tina, Beth, Kathleen, Heather, Gordon, Stan, Linda B, Linda G, Maria, Dee, Elena, and special thanks to Dean, Kay1, Kay2, Bob, Amy, and Laura.

To McCourt, Vonna, and Sara for the manuscript read-throughts at the Darcy Pattison workshop.

Special thanks to Deb Adams and Mary Saums for the ongoing inspiration and support.

Thanks to Paul, the ever-patient man who keeps me going.

CHAPTER ONE

The crisp air of the late Maryland spring brushed my cheeks as I cued Cricket for her left canter lead. Making a balanced turn in the corner, I sighted on the freshly painted Pony Club jump in the middle of the arena.

"Oxer!" I called out to let everyone know which obstacle we planned to take.

Another rider circled to get out of our way. Cricket took it clear. It was only two-feet six, and the spread between the poles was not very wide. The size didn't matter. My heart beat faster every time I let go of everything but that one moment: the even strides into the jump, the pure joy of flying through the air on this amazing chestnut mare, and the rush of landing safely on the other side.

As we approached the next jump I mentally crossed my fingers. For some reason Cricket thought blue plastic barrels would eat her. Three of them lay on their side under the rail. Two strides out, the mare shifted her weight. A trickle of acid hit my stomach. *Deep breath. Right rein tug-and-release to steer Cricket back into the jump.* "Stay straight." I heard myself say out loud. And even had a chance to think it would work.

Then Cricket shied hard. My hope for a clear round dissolved into slow motion disaster. The impact with the jump threw me forward onto Cricket's mane.

The world went sideways.

Cricket screeched to a halt. I made like a monkey, clinging to the underside of her neck. I lowered my feet to the ground, glad I hadn't kissed the dirt this time. My mare's neck felt warm and scratchy under my fingers as I patted her neck to reassure us both that we were okay.

"You're getting better at falling with style, Sophie," my trainer, Queenie Ashe, said. The tiny woman adjusted her beloved Baltimore Orioles baseball cap as she walked over to the fallen uprights. Queenie righted the jump standard and lifted the wooden pole out of the arena sand to fit it back into the cups. As she straightened, she caught sight of my face.

"You all right?" she asked.

I turned and fiddled with Cricket's bridle. "Cricket's mane got in my eyes was all," I said. At almost thirteen, I was far too old to cry over a silly refusal. But there I was, tears in my eyes, my blonde complexion probably showing every red inch of my mortification.

Show Jump Rally, the Pony Club competition I'd been waiting for all year, was two weeks away. Too bad Pony Club didn't award ribbons for falling with style. We'd get first place. As it was, maybe I ought to stay home to avoid embarrassing myself to death. Cricket would go over the blue barrels for Queenie and for my best friend, Yasmine Sengupta. But not for me—who gave her treats, and groomed her, and made sure her stall was clean and comfortable.

I wanted to sniffle and howl like I was two. Instead, I fit my boot into the stirrup and swung back up in the saddle. Queenie handed me my water bottle.

"Take a deep breath," she advised.

I took a slug of cold water and felt the heat in my cheeks ease.

"In, two, three, four. Out, two, three, four." I counted silently as I breathed. Queenie's method helped, just like it always did.

Yasmine rode by on Bourbon, one of the other lesson horses.

"You almost did it that time," she called.

"Thanks," I said. I reached forward and poured half the bottle on Cricket's neck to help her cool off a little.

"Remember, if riding were easy, everyone would be a champion. Only the ones who keep trying and learn from their mistakes make it that far." Queenie's sun-weathered lines around her grey eyes deepened as she smiled. Her weathered hand stroked the damp chestnut hair on Cricket's neck. "You've made a lot of progress since you leased Cricket."

"Half leased," I reminded her. I tried to smile back but couldn't quite pull it off. There were a ton of people in the arena. They'd all just seen me make a total fool of myself.

"Riding her four times a week has made a huge difference for you. Don't knock what ya got."

I wasn't being ungrateful. Mom worked hard to pay for that half-lease.

Cricket skittered a little to one side when the third pair in our lesson group, Tanner Everett, and his huge black Shire/Thoroughbred cross, Vee, knocked over a heavy standard. Without the side support, the poles fell to the ground with a loud crash.

Tanner circled around and called out, "Wish I could ride this tank like you ride your girl," he called.

I instantly felt better. Vee was always difficult; Cricket was usually wonderful. It was just that one darn jump. The smile I'd reached for came more easily this time. Tanner was pretty nice, one of the few boys I knew who had the sense to like horses. Not as cute as the new boy working at Dry Creek Riding School though. Luis Cramer was sixteen, not too much older than I was, and I had a serious crush on him.

I looked around to see if Luis had seen me fall. I breathed easier when I didn't see him.

Queenie gathered us in the middle of the arena, led our usual end-of-lesson discussion, then dismissed us.

The clock at the entrance to the arena said five-thirty. Almost time to go home. Mom and Mrs. Sengupta carpooled on the days we went to Dry Creek. Yasmine's mom picked us up from school and dropped us off at the barn. Mom picked us up after she finished work. Except for Tuesday, my personal favorite day of the week. Riding lesson and a ride home with Mom's favorite brother, Uncle Charlie, all in one day. He shod horses for many of the boarders at Dry Creek that afternoon. Queenie said he was the best farrier around.

Now that the lesson was over, Cricket needed to cool down. My fingers opened so that the reins slipped through a little at a time. As the mare felt the bit loosen in her mouth, she lengthened her stride and dropped her head so that her back stretched. Cricket snorted a little, and followed up with a whinny that made the saddle vibrate. My hand smoothed the hair on her damp neck. Yasmine let her horse have a long rein too, steering Bourbon for the rail so we could walk together. After a slow circuit, I opened my inside rein, cueing Cricket to turn across the arena so that she could stretch her other side.

A sudden shout rang out from behind me. Tanner's horse shot by. Cricket swung sideways to get out of the way and rammed my leg against the pipe-fence rail.

I forgot all about my leg when Tanner hit the ground about twenty feet past us. Queenie ran toward him, calling out, "Loose horse!" as she went. The gelding slowed to a trot as he got close to the end of the arena. The toot did a fancy side-pass all the way from the corner to the gate—anything rather than jump. Once outside the arena, the horse headed straight toward the barn, slowing to a trot when he got close.

Luis came out of the wide doorway, a wheelbarrow rolling along in front of him. He dropped the handles and reached out to snag the horse's reins. Vee stopped when he felt the tug on his mouth and swung around to face his captor. The gelding settled as Luis stroked the horse's sweaty neck.

I reached down and rubbed my sore knee as I admired Luis's horse-handling skills. Cute and good with horses. Perfect guy.

Tanner's mom came out of the barn. When Mrs. Everett saw Tanner sitting in the dirt she started running. Moms always think getting there fast will help once you've already hit the ground.

Mrs. Everett arrived just as Queenie helped Tanner up. "Where are you?"

Tanner didn't quite roll his eyes, but I could tell it was a close thing.

"I didn't hit my head that hard," he said.

"You know the drill," Queenie said. "Concussions are no laughing matter." She looked in both his eyes. Then she held up a couple of fingers and asked him to tell her how many.

"Four," he said. "Really, I'm fine."

Queenie frowned and shook her head at him.

"How many?" The trainer held up her fingers again.

Tanner sighed. "Two." He unsnapped the harness of his helmet and handed it to the trainer.

Queenie rolled the helmet over until the side where his head had hit the dirt was on top. "He's going to need a new helmet," she said to Mrs. Everett. "Good thing you own a tack shop."

Mrs. Everett and her brother, Mr. Nelson, owned the store where my mom worked as the bookkeeper. Still, I understood when Mrs. Everett winced. Helmets are not cheap.

"You didn't do this when Sophie fell," Tanner said.

Queenie's eyes narrowed. "Sophie didn't hit her head. You did. You'll just have to forgive me for caring."

As Tanner and his mom walked away, I heard her say, "You all right?"

"Mom, please. I'm not broken," Tanner said.

Mrs. Everett put a hand out like she was going to put her arm around him, but then let it drop to her side as they walked back toward the barn.

Thank goodness. The only thing more embarrassing than getting tossed off your horse is when your mom goes all hovery on you.

When they got back to the barn, Tanner went on in. I noticed that even though he'd said he was fine, his left leg looked pretty lame to me.

Mrs. Everett walked over to Luis, who still held Vee. She snatched the reins away from him and spoke to him like she wanted to pull him to pieces. Luis looked like he wanted to hit her. Instead he turned on his heel and pushed the wheelbarrow out toward the manure spreader. Mrs. Everett turned and yanked the horse into the barn.

What was that all about? I wondered.

She must have been really rattled by Tanner's fall to be so mean to Luis. Although Mom had said Mrs. Everett had been really grumpy lately. Maybe it wasn't just Tanner's fall that had her jumping out of her skin.

Fortunately, Mrs. Everett's bad mood was not my problem. After a few steps of the steady one-two-three-four rhythm of my mare's walk, Cricket and I caught up with Yasmine and Bourbon. She looked back over her shoulder and shrugged. "Poor Tanner."

I nodded agreement. He'd wanted to keep leasing Skittles, Queenie's piebald pony who jumped like a fiend. Most of us kids leased or half-leased horses rather than buying our own. They were expensive enough just to rent. I couldn't imagine us ever having enough money to own a horse.

A rider cantered by and called out, "Inside."

Cricket and I dropped back behind Bourbon and Yasmine to give them room to pass. The tip of my friend's sleek black fishtail-braid ticked off the horse's rhythm like the pendulum on Uncle Charlie's grandfather clock. I wished I had long straight hair like her. Mine was always a snarl of dark blonde curls, all determined to escape my ponytail holder.

"Ready to go?" she asked.

I put my hand down on Cricket's neck.

"Yeah. Cricket's cool enough. How about Bourbon?"

"He's good too," Yasmine said.

We followed the arena fence back to the exit gate. Tanner and his mom stood outside the arena. I tried not to stare as she grabbed Tanner by the arm and dragged him out to the parking lot.

CHAPTER TWO

Queenie pulled me aside before we left to let me know that the girl who had the other half-lease on Cricket was moving away. When she added that I could get a discount if I mucked stalls every afternoon, I couldn't wait to get home and talk to Mom. Perfect timing. With Uncle Charlie there for dinner, Mom would be in a good mood.

After we put the horses back in their stalls for the night, Yasmine and I scrambled into Uncle Charlie's old blue F-150. He climbed in the driver's side and off we went. The metal rasps and nippers in his farrier toolbox in the truck bed jangled each time we went over a bump.

The truck pulled into Yasmine's driveway. She lived close to our school. I lived in an old farmhouse across the marsh from her neighborhood. If we both leaned out our windows we could almost see each other.

"Good luck," my friend whispered before she ran into her house.

We backed out of the drive and headed to my house. Uncle Charlie told me a funny story about a horse he'd seen that morning who had gotten stuck in the owner's pond. Pretty soon he had me laughing about what should have been a scary story.

We turned onto Greer Dairy Road and our gravel drive came into view. He pulled in and steered the truck around to the back. Mom came to the kitchen door.

"Charlie," she called. "Stay for supper?"

Uncle Charlie pretended to think about it. "I guess."

Like he ever turned down chicken and dumplings. Uncle Charlie wasn't married, and he didn't have kids. He told me once that having this Tuesday dinner with family was the most important thing he did all week. I pulled the handle on the door and got out.

We took the short set of stairs onto the enclosed back porch. I stopped to take off my paddock boots. Mom hated it when I tracked barn dirt on her kitchen floor. I tossed them next to the washer. That done, I followed him in the back door.

Misty, our old golden retriever, went wild. She loved Uncle Charlie as much as Mom and I do. The small throw rug in front of the sink skidded out from under her feet as the dog launched herself at my uncle.

Mom turned from the open fridge, tripped on the crumpled rug, and dropped the milk carton. Spilled milk spread across the floor. Misty abandoned Uncle Charlie for the milk puddle. Her tongue lapped at the spreading stain.

"Fickle hound," Uncle Charlie laughed.

Mom picked up a tea towel to use as a mop. "For goodness sake, Sophie, take that dog upstairs with you while I clean that up."

"She's doing a good job." I bounced on my toes, bursting with the news about Cricket.

"Speaking of cleaning," Mom started.

I grabbed Misty's collar and hauled her behind me. I was halfway up the stairs before Mom could tell me to clean my room like she always did. No need to get her upset before I had a chance to ask her for the biggest thing ever.

"We'll eat in fifteen minutes," Mom called after me.

I peeled off my socks and tossed them on the pile of dirty clothes on my floor. The warped dresser drawer protested when I went to get clean jeans and a t-shirt.

Clean clothes in hand, I used my knee to keep Misty in my room as I closed the door. It was only a few steps to the bathroom. A few minutes later I'd scrubbed myself clean, washed my hair, and dressed.

Once in the hall, a scorched smell hit me. I frowned. Mom burning dinner? That hadn't happened since the bad days during the divorce. For a second, I forgot all about my good news. My stomach churned.

A few steps to the left so I could throw the rest of my dirty clothes at the pile on the floor and let Misty out. I could clean up after I found out what was going on. The dog led the way down the stairs.

I arrived in the kitchen door to find Mom bent over the stove saying words that would have gotten me grounded for a month.

"It's not my store, so it's not my call. But my two cents? Paying for Nancy Everett to take a fancy buying trip instead of ordering from catalogues like we usually do is wrong, Charlie. It's just wrong." Mom finished up.

I couldn't believe she burned dinner over work stuff. My stomach rumbled.

"Dinner still okay?" I asked.

Mom and Uncle Charlie exchanged glances as I walked in. I could almost see them slam the door on their discussion.

"It'll taste fine," Mom said.

"I hope so, I'm starving."

"Sophie Marie, don't you take that tone with me," Mom said.

What was with her? I walked over and yanked open the silverware drawer. Feeling only slightly better, I stomped over to the table and put knives, forks, and spoons at our places, grabbed napkins and folded them under the fork, then turned to see if Mom had noticed what a good job I'd done despite how hurt I was.

Neither Mom nor Uncle Charlie paid any attention to me. Mom had her back to me as she pulled soup bowls out of the cupboard. My uncle stirred the pot with an old wooden spoon. He pulled up a sample, blew across it, then tasted it.

"Not terrible," he said to Mom.

He snagged the ladle from the crock next to the stove and filled the waiting bowls.

Mom gave Misty a stern look as she filled glasses with water. She might have half-smiled at Uncle Charlie for his remark about the food, but she was still in a mood. I went over and sat down. The lease talk I wanted to have with mom would go way better if she didn't think I was sulking over her snapping at me.

Mom set the waters by our places. Uncle Charlie brought over the bowls.

We said grace.

Uncle Charlie was right. Dinner wasn't horrible. It's wasn't good though. The chicken tasted like it had been in the pot for a week. Dumplings were rubber. And even though Mom and Uncle Charlie had stopped talking about the work stuff, they still acted weird.

If I was going to talk to Mom about the lease, I needed to lighten her up. I kept quiet about the food, and thought, and thought. Finally, I hit on just the right thing to talk about.

"Ingrid tried out for cheerleading today."

Mom's fingers tightened on her fork. "You aren't back to being friends again after the way she treated you?"

Ingrid had been my best friend and a good rider until she fell and broke her arm.

Then she'd just quit. Quit riding. Quit being my friend.

Worse, Ingrid had started making fun of me in school. She'd never been one of Mom's favorite people. When I'd come home crying about stuff Ingrid had done, well, Mom couldn't stand her after that.

"Not in this lifetime." I got back to my story. "Tryouts were in the gym. Coach Allison kept telling her to go to the other end."

"Why?" Uncle Charlie asked.

"Basketball try-outs were at the same time," I said.

Mom tried to smother a laugh. She failed. Ingrid was five-ten.

"Coach Allison put her on the basketball team, didn't she?" Mom asked.

"Ingrid was so mad." I grinned. "Now she has to break a sweat."

I pushed my plate back and folded my napkin. Now that I'd coaxed Mom into a good mood...

"Mom, Cricket's lease is open next month."

Mom didn't answer. I scooted to the front of my chair.

"Queenie said—"

Mom held up one hand, palm out.

That meant her answer was no.

"But Queenie said I could work off part of the cost!" Mom needed to know that I was going to help pay for this.

"We can't," she said.

"But..." I began.

"The answer is no, young lady. End of discussion."

Hand shaking, I reached for Uncle Charlie's plate. If Mom wouldn't talk about it, I might as well get started on the dishes. The brass faucet handle was cold against my even colder hand.

Mom came up beside me. She put her plate down on the counter. Her hand settled on my shoulder. "I know how important this is to you. I planned on asking for a raise so that we could afford this."

"I'll never get over those stupid blue barrels if I only ride four times a week." My voice was as dry as the burned chicken had been.

I felt her look at Uncle Charlie and turned my head toward him too. His face was twisted into an expression I'd never seen there before.

"They're taking advantage of you," Uncle Charlie said.

He was talking about work stuff again.

I looked at Mom.

She took her hand off my shoulder and waved away his suggestion. "The Nelsons are good people. They're struggling is all."

Mom turned back to me. "Don asked me to take a cut in pay. Profits have been off lately."

Nelson's Tack was always packed with customers. Mr. Nelson, Don to Mom, always said Mom was the best bookkeeper on the planet. Why would they cut her pay?

Another thought occurred to me, and this one made my hands shake.

"Does this mean we can't lease Cricket at all?" I leaned on the counter when my knees went wobbly.

"I'll make sure you get to keep riding, even if we have to cut back some-place else," Mom said.

My knees still wobbled, but I felt better enough to stick a couple of fingers under the water stream while I thought about what Mom had said—and what she hadn't said.

The water warmed. I stuck the rubber stopper in the drain and squirted dish soap in. Lavender-scented suds rose as I slid the dishes into the water.

"I'll do that," Mom said. She handed me a dish towel to dry my hands.

I looked up at her. She never offered to do the dishes.

"Go on, Sophie. Your mom and I need to have a grown-up talk." Uncle's Charlie's words stung.

Grown up talk. Like I was too little to think straight.

Mom crossed her arms over her chest when I opened my mouth to speak and then tilted her head at the door. Mad again.

She wasn't the only one. I might have stomped a little bit on my way out.

Misty stayed behind, which stung.

Once upstairs, I shoved the dirty clothes over in the corner of my room and dumped my books out of my backpack. They made a satisfying thud as they struck the floor.

"Sophie!" Mom's voice filtered through the floorboards.

Lips pursed, I blew her a raspberry. The kitchen was right below my room. Like I didn't know that when I dumped my books.

I fished out *A Day No Pigs Would Die.* We had a test coming up the follow-ing Monday. I needed to read the assigned chapters. Opening my closet door, I flipped the extra blanket off the foot of my bed and threw it over the pile of clothes on the floor inside. Plopping down, I opened the book and read until my eyes crossed. I wasn't feeling it.

I picked up my phone and called Yasmine.

She didn't answer. A second later I got a text that said, "Talking to Tan-ner!!!!!!"

Great. Mom shut me out and my best friend was more interested in talking to a boy than me. Sure, Tanner was pretty cool, and Yasmine had a crush the size of Montana on him. He was just a boy. I was her best friend.

"CALL ME BACK," I texted. Hopefully she could tell by the all caps that this was important.

"'K," she replied.

I dropped the phone and eyed the bookshelf on the back wall. Dad had built the bookcase to disguise the door to the crawl space, transforming it into my very own secret room. I'd stopped using it when Dad left for California. The floor of my closet was plenty big enough to make a cozy place to read. For one thing, the crawl space wasn't heated. For another, going in there made me miss Dad more than I already did.

I thought about calling him to ask for money for Cricket's lease, but decided not to. Mom and Dad both got mad the last time I tried something like that. They didn't get along all the time, what with Dad feeling like I should come out there more often to see him and Mom backing me up when I wanted to spend time with my friends. Summers and the winter school break were enough to be spending in a place where I knew exactly one person. Especially since that person had to go to work for most of the day. But if Mom said no, and I called Dad, it was like they were still married or something. Instant trouble for me if I went behind her back.

I raised up on my knees to look at the shelves. They were crammed full of my childhood horse books. *Misty of Chincoteague*, of course. My *Horses and Friends* books. Every single one of the little kid Pony Pal series. I pulled out the first one. Once opened, I got wrapped up in it. Gotta love a story where all the problems could be solved from the time you opened the book to the time you finished.

I got mad when Yasmine still hadn't called back by the time I closed the book. I got up and stretched. My bed called my name. I snuggled in and made a cocoon out of my blankets.

When Mom came in to tell me it was time to go to sleep, she found me snuggled up with a pile of my old books. I didn't tell her I'd never gotten around to reading the homework assignment. I promised myself that I would do that on the bus to school.

CHAPTER THREE

Yasmine finally called back about nine-thirty. Her mom had taken her phone away when she found out she was talking to a boy. She had to wait until Mrs. Sengupta was watching her favorite show before she could sneak down and get her phone.

Once we'd talked about how depressed I was about my situation with Cricket, we talked about Tanner and school. Fortunately, Yasmine had read the chapters in the *Pig* book. She gave me a "Spark Notes" synopsis of the reading.

After we hung up, I rolled onto my back and wondered when I would have a boyfriend I could get caught talking to late at night. Probably be awhile. Crushing on Luis was enough for me. Figuring out how to make that full lease happen was way more important. I sat up and hugged myself. Queenie'd offered to let me clean stalls to help pay for the full lease. Maybe she'd let me clean tack too, and that might be enough to get the full lease without Mom having to pay more.

Breakfast the next morning was one of the quietest ever. Mom was in a bad mood again. I didn't say anything about the lease because I wanted to talk to Queenie first. Mom couldn't say no if I was going to earn the difference.

When I went out to catch the bus, Mom didn't look up from the shop's accounting pages she'd brought home with her. I ignored my hurt feelings. I was too old for good-bye hugs anyway.

Once on the bus, I pulled out my book and read most of the first chapter. That and Yasmine's help turned out to be enough to get me through the class discussion in English. My other classes were quiet enough that I finished several Tack Cleaner For Hire signs with my phone number. I'd show them to Queenie that afternoon and start earning money right away.

After school, Yasmine and I joined the throng of kids waiting for rides outside the gym. Teachers stood by the waiting cars. They were supposed to make sure we went home with the right parents. Like we'd be stupid enough to get a car with a stranger?

Mrs. Sengupta was third in line. We hopped in, and off we went.

When we got to the barn, we thanked Yasmine's mom for the ride, and went on inside. Georgia, the girl who shared Cricket's lease with me, had the mare on Wednesday, but I always went to hang out. Yasmine had a full lease on Bourbon. Normally, I didn't mind. That day? Different story.

I went to find Queenie. It felt like a blow to my stomach when the assistant trainer told me Queenie had gone to trailer some stranded horses back to the barn while the owner took care of their broken-down truck. Shoving the fliers back inside my backpack, I went and stashed it in the tack room, then went to watch Yasmine ride.

I kicked a rock out of my way as Georgia led Cricket over to the mounting block and got on. They moved off across the arena. The mare tossed her head every other stride, proof that she didn't like Georgia as much as she did me. I took a seat on the top rail of the arena and tried not to mind that someone else was riding my horse.

Yasmine practiced some of the things we'd done in our lesson the day before, and I imagined doing them on Cricket. My friend looked more relaxed in the saddle than she had in awhile. Tanner wasn't there. With his Mom on that buying trip, he must've had to stay home from the barn.

Yasmine and Bourbon stopped next to me. I handed her the water bottle off the top of the fence post.

"Ready?" I asked.

"Bourbon's nearly cool," Yasmine said. "Another pass around the arena and I'll be ready to go groom him."

To my surprise, I heard Mom calling my name. I turned and saw her walking my way.

Yasmine and Bourbon moved on.

Good. She was there while Georgia was riding. I could point out to Mom how tense Cricket was with a rider who wasn't *me*.

Then she got close enough that I could see her face. She was really upset. Way worse than she had been the night before.

"Mom?"

"Good, you haven't heard. I wanted to tell you myself," Mom said. "Nelson's burned down this morning."

Mom looked okay, but I still jumped down off the fence for a closer look. Where was she hurt? Her curly blonde hair was messy. Black mascara smudged the hollows under both eyes. No bandages though.

"What happened?" I asked, once I knew that she was fine.

"Nobody knows for sure yet how the fire started. Most of the store is a total loss."

"Everyone's okay, right?" I asked.

"Mr. Nelson is fine, Mrs. Nelson is in the hospital with some burns on her hands. We tried to keep her from going back in, but the store cat was trapped in the office. She got Tom-Kitten out."

Please let the store cat be all right. "Is he..." I couldn't even finish the question. Tom-Kitten was legendary. Everyone loved that little guy.

"His fur is a little short on one side, but he's going to be fine."

I breathed a sigh of relief over Tom-Kitten and that the Nelsons weren't badly injured. Poor Brandon and Brigitte, having their mom hurt like that. The Nelson twins were Yasmine's and my personal shadows at the barn and at Pony Club events. They were really cute.

I looked up in time to see that funny expression show up again and settle in around Mom's eyes. I opened my mouth to ask her what else was wrong when Yasmine rode up.

"Hi, Mrs. Allen," she said to Mom. "What's up?"

"Oh Jazzy," Mom replied, using Yasmine's hated childhood nickname. "I was just telling Sophie some bad news." Mom quickly ran through the whole story.

Yasmine's normally brown face turned ashy grey as she listened. "That's horrible."

Mom made a sound of protest, drawing my attention back to her. Her hand shook as she reached out to grip the fence. "Honey, we need to go."

"I promised Yasmine I would help her put Bourbon up," I protested.

"We're leaving now," Mom said.

I frowned. Mom was almost as obsessive as Queenie about taking proper care of the horses. She always let me help Yasmine. Always.

"Mom?" I began.

Mom's hand spasmed as she gripped the pipe of the fence, knuckles turning dead white. "For once in your life, Sophie Marie Allen, do *what* I tell you *when* I tell you."

I backed away. The color drained from Mom's face as she looked over my shoulder at the barn. I turned to see what had spooked her.

Mrs. Everett stood outside the dressage barn talking with a couple of boarders. The expression on her face was pure poison. She pointed at Mom. Shocked looks burst out on the boarders' faces. Mrs. Everett nodded as if to confirm whatever it was that she had just said.

My head whipped around. There were tears in the corners of Mom's eyes.

"What is going on?" I asked. "Wasn't she supposed to be out of town?"

Mom tugged my arm in the direction of the parking lot as she gave me what I'm sure she thought was a brave look. "She came back when she got to the call about the fire. C'mon. We have to leave before this gets ugly."

I heard the crunch of boots coming closer through the arena sand.

Mrs. Everett stopped across the fence from my mom. Mom took a step back as if she was afraid of her. "How could you?" Mrs. Everett said.

Bourbon danced a step away as Yasmine gasped.

"Ron knows I didn't do it," Mom said.

Mr. Nelson knew Mom didn't do what?

"The fire marshal said that the fire started at your desk."

The fire marshal? Like the one Mom always threatened to call when my room got out of control? I must have said something, because Mom shoved me behind her and Mrs. Everett transferred her attention to me.

Yasmine retreated. She pointed Bourbon at the arena gate and picked up a trot. I wished I could go with her.

Mom spoke. Mrs. Everett's gaze snapped back to her. "It may have, but not because I set it. You know better, or will once you calm down and think about it. Until then, you need to keep your opinions to yourself. I saw you over there, telling those women who knows what!" Each word was bitten off short and crisp. I hadn't seen Mom this riled up for a long time, not since the time I walked all the way down to the Heavenly Waters, the little stream down the road from our house all by myself when I was only four. Mom had been scared then. So scared she got mad as fire. I took a good hard look at my mother. She *was* angry—wasn't she?

"You won't get away with this." Mrs. Everett's face hardened as she wheeled and stalked away.

"Mom?" I said.

"I'm sorry." Mom glared in Mrs. Everett's direction. "That...well, I can't call her what I really want to." She transferred her attention back to me. "I wanted to tell you myself. Preliminary signs are that the fire started at my desk."

I frowned. "But..."

"Nancy Everett blames the first person to cross her path for whatever's going wrong," Mom said. "It's not like she was even there to know what happened. She didn't even get back from her buying trip until after the fire was out."

"Okay," I said, because there really wasn't anything else I could think of that wouldn't sound disrespectful.

Cricket went by, so crooked from the girl's strong hand on her right rein that I wanted to scream. I looked back at the barn and saw Yasmine and Bourbon outside. My friend dismounted and looked my way as if to say, Coming?"

"Can I go tell Yasmine good-bye?"

"I'll come with you."

"That's okay. I'll meet you at the car." I needed a minute to figure this out.

Mom looked at me. She reached out and smoothed my hair back from my face. "Stay away from Mrs. Everett."

No kidding. I did not intend to cross paths with her. I nodded and went to join Yasmine in Bourbon's stall.

"You all right?" she asked. She pulled the saddle from Bourbon's back and set it on the rack outside the stall.

"Sure," I said. "I love being yelled at in front of everybody."

"Liar." Yasmine tossed her head. She took a closer look at my expression. "Don't tell me you're worried about all that. No one who knows your mom will believe it."

As we groomed Bourbon, a couple of boarders looked in the stall as they passed. The whispers began when they were a few steps down the aisle. My jaw clenched. Yasmine was wrong.

"I'd better go," I said.

"Can you put Bourbon's tack up on your way to the car?" my friend asked.

"Sure." I picked up the saddle and bridle and left Yasmine brushing the horse. Hopefully Mom wouldn't be too mad.

Georgia was in the tack room putting Cricket's saddle and bridle away when I got there.

"Heard you had to move," I said.

"Yeah. We move a lot."

"Cricket will miss you." Didn't hurt me any to tell her that white lie. When she wasn't riding my mare she seemed like a pretty nice girl.

"We have to leave in two weeks," Georgia said. She started to cry. Covering her face with one hand, she turned and ran for the bathroom.

I walked down to Cricket's stall. Mom was waiting on me, but I needed a minute alone with the horse. My mare nickered a welcome. Her velvet nose sniffed at my hands, searching for treats. Since I was empty-handed, she went back to her hay. I leaned in and put my cheek against Cricket's warm neck. Her hide had that wonderful smell that made everything seem like it would turn out all right. I felt for Georgia. Moving and losing your horse would be the worst possible thing ever. As long as I had Cricket, nothing else mattered.

Two women walked by.

"I heard they found evidence."

"I don't believe it. She's so nice, and her little girl is great with her horse."

"There was a huge fight yesterday in the store. Money's missing." The woman's voice harshened. "I was there. And I have to say that Jamie Allen's always had a temper on her."

Jamie Allen. My mother.

The voices faded away. My hands shook as I stepped toward the front of the stall. A movement caught my eye. It was Mom, pressed back into the shadows of the feed room catty-corner from where I stood. What I saw frightened me right down to my toes. Mom didn't look like she did when I talked back to her or like when she and Dad argued about their divorce. Her expression was exactly the same one she wore when I caught her smoking behind the house after she promised to quit. My mother looked guilty.

CHAPTER FOUR

The hall was crowded before first period the next morning. I'd almost fought my way to my locker when a hand struck between my shoulder blades. I slammed into the metal doors next to me. I whipped around. The girl who'd shoved me stood a foot away, arms laced around a stack of books. Ingrid of course. My former best friend who'd just made the basketball team. The kids across the hall turned and stared.

"Your mom was always mean to me, even when we were friends. I'm not surprised she burned down the tack shop," Ingrid said.

"She did not!" I answered.

Ingrid tossed her head. The gesture flipped her shoulder-length auburn hair back away from her face. She'd started doing that when her growth spurt made her taller than most of the rest of us.

The bigger girl put her hands on her hips and loomed over me. "One. She's got the temper. Two. She was about to get fired. Do the math," Ingrid said.

"She's not going to jail." Yasmine, a tiny spitfire in blue, flew in and pushed Ingrid. The taller girl's load of books crashed to the floor.

My new best friend was way better than my old one.

I leaned down and picked up Ingrid's pre-algebra book.

"Here." I hurled the text at Ingrid like a basketball pass. "You might need this. Although I doubt you've had time enough to study. You probably spent the whole night on the phone talking about something you know nothing about."

Ingrid's fingers grabbed the book out of the air. She cradled it to her chest. "Pop quiz?" she groaned.

I grinned at her, and put every ounce of anger I had behind my bared teeth. Even Yasmine backed off a step.

"Yup." I paused for effect. "And Ingrid, you suck at math."

My lunch sack rustled as I sat it next to Kilby Solomon's school lunch tray. I took a quick look at her food. All yellow, Kilby's favorite color. She even ate the yellow M&Ms first. That was so wrong. Everyone knew the red ones were the best.

I dumped my lunch out of the bag. Baloney sandwich. Mom knew I hated baloney. Had to be punishment for taking so long at the barn the night before.

I eyed Kilby's tray.

"Want to trade?" I asked.

"For what?"

I pointed at her apple.

"Sure!" Good thing Kilby had two friends who always brought lunch. Yasmine or I always had something to share or trade. She'd've starved if she'd had to eat the mystery meat on her lunch tray.

"I'm sorry about Ingrid," Kilby said.

"She said what everyone thinks," I said.

"Not everyone," she said.

I would have given her my sandwich for nothing after that. Still, Kilby had braces. She couldn't eat the apple. I took a bite.

Yasmine scooted into the seat across from me.

"Where's Justine?" she asked. Justine McGrath and Kilby had eaten lunch with me since the middle of fifth grade when Ingrid decided I wasn't cool anymore. Yasmine moved to Maryland as school started and we sat next to each other in our first class. She fit right in.

"In line. Must have forgotten her lunch again," I said.

Yasmine opened her lunchbox. She pulled out two peanut butter and jelly sandwiches. She looked at them for a minute and then puffed her cheeks out like an outraged squirrel.

We grinned at each other. We could never figure out why Mrs. Sengupta sent two PB & J's every day. Yasmine was tiny. No way could she eat that much. Yasmine looked at Kilby and saw her eating my sandwich. She pushed her extra over to Justine's place.

I bit into the apple. Nice and crisp and juicy. I felt a pang. Should have saved it for Cricket.

The clatter of a plastic tray hitting the table heralded Justine's arrival. "Sophie, I heard about Ingrid. She is so stupid. I know it looks bad for your mom, but I'm sure she won't be in jail long—"

The apple lodged in my throat. I coughed, tried to breathe, then coughed again.

Kilby pounded my back while Yasmine lit into Justine.

I shoved my way away from the table and ran for the water fountain outside the cafeteria.

The hall monitor didn't even question me. I dove for the handle and gulped down about a gallon of water. The feeling of suffocation eased. I released the knob. Water dripped from my cheeks. Hands braced against either side of the fountain. I sucked in a shaky breath.

"What happened?" a guy asked behind me.

"Food got stuck in my throat," I said.

I took another short drink and straightened. The guy was Tanner.

"Come to gloat?" I asked. The back of my hand dashed the remaining water away from my face.

"What? No. I saw you... I mean..." Tanner's words spluttered to silence.

"Your mom is telling lies," I said.

"She's not lying," he said.

I almost punched him. "So you think my mother burned down the place she works?

"Mom says—" Tanner started to say.

"I don't care what your mom says." The memory of Mom's expression the night before made my voice crack. She'd looked guilty. What if she was?

Tanner's words dried up about then. That was lucky. If he'd said anything at that moment, there was no telling what I would have done.

"Mom says I can't have lessons with you and Yasmine anymore," he finally said.

I felt like he'd slammed me against the wall.

"Is that all you can think about?" I said. "Who's in your ride group? No store means no job for my mom. We won't have any money." My breath hitched as I realized what that could mean. My worst nightmare might come true! No money, no Cricket.

"Must be nice to be you." I spat out. "You don't have to worry about a single thing except who you ride with."

Tanner's face drained of color. He took a step back and looked at me like he had never seen me before. "Your family isn't the only one with money trouble." Tanner stopped and swallowed hard. "I can't ride with you and Yasmine anymore because Dad says we have to sell Vee. No store means no money for us too."

"I didn't know," I whispered.

This time it was my throat that closed up. We both had to give up our horses. But only I had been mean.

The bell rang. Streams of kids flowed out of the cafeteria, separating the two of us before I could say anything more.

Yasmine and I left pre-algebra at the same time.

"How did you know Mrs. Sturman would spring a pop quiz?" she demanded.

"I didn't." I said. "What's worse is that I bet Ingrid did better than I did. Saw her studying those stupid equations during History."

"Ouch!" Yasmine said.

"Tell me about it. Listen," I said. "Can your mom pick you up from the barn? Mom isn't feeling too well. I think I'll just go home."

Yasmine tossed her braid and looked sideways at me. "You afraid to go to the barn after the way people treated you yesterday?" she asked.

"Not exactly." I was, but admitting it seemed chicken.

"Your mom wouldn't want you to skip riding," Yasmine said.

Mom wouldn't want me getting made fun of either.

Yasmine wouldn't leave it alone. In the end, both of us were in our usual pickup spot outside the gym. Ingrid came out with some of her new shmancy friends. Her mom's BMW was at the front of the line. Ingrid stuck her tongue out at me as they pulled away. Lame.

"Tanner has to sell Vee," I said.

"No way," Yasmine said. "That horrible. If I owned Bourbon, there would be no way I'd let my parents sell him."

"Same with Cricket," I said. I was glad for the first time since I started riding the mare that I didn't own her. Not being able to ride Queenie's horse wasn't the same as having to sell her to a stranger.

"Is Tanner okay?" Yasmine asked.

"Well..." I scuffed the edge of my flip-flop on the sidewalk. "I don't think he's talking to me anymore."

"He's probably just embarrassed about how his mom treated you yesterday," Yasmine said. "He'll get over it."

"I don't think so." I made myself tell Yasmine what I'd said. For the very first time, my best friend's anger was trained on me.

It was a relief when Mrs. Sengupta pulled up. We piled in.

The ride out to the farm took forever. Mrs. Sengupta kept up a steady patter of words. She didn't even notice how quiet the backseat was. I caught Yasmine giving me her narrow-eyed, "I'm really mad" look. I crossed my arms over my chest and turned away. Sure, I wasn't proud of how I'd reacted. But if I lost Yasmine over a guy, now, when I really needed my best friend, it would be as bad as losing Cricket. The minute the car was in PARK we shot out of the car.

"Thanks," we said, as I slammed the door. Yasmine and I headed inside.

Once inside and out of sight, I put a hand out and stopped Yasmine.

"I'm going to apologize to Tanner," I told her.

"You'd better," she said. She tilted her head to one side and considered me.

I held my breath. It whooshed out when her mouth quirked up.

"I'll go find Tanner and tell him you want to talk," Yasmine said.

"Okay," I said.

Yasmine went to the tack room to get her stuff.

I headed to the bathroom. Someone rattled the doorknob before I'd even had a chance to change my jeans.

"Just a minute," I called out. The day was hotter than usual for April. I lifted the hair from the back of my neck and fastened it into a pony tail with a hair tie I had fished out of my backpack.

"Let me in," Yasmine said, rattling the door.

Good thing I was still dressed. She hadn't wasted any time.

I flipped the lock. Yasmine pushed me back inside and shut the door.

Yasmine's breath hissed like an angry cat. "You are not going to believe this." Then she proceeded to hyperventilate a little more.

"I can't '*not* believe it' until you tell me what it was," I prompted.

When she didn't speak, I wanted to scream. Instead I grabbed her arms and shook her. "What?"

"Mrs. Everett says she has evidence that your mom set the fire."

"She can't," I said. My voice quavered like it did in school when I wasn't sure I had the right answer. The women the night before had mentioned evidence. Surely it wasn't real.

Pity grew in my friend's dark brown eyes.

I looked away.

My best friend should know better. Mom had nothing to do with this. There were lots of other people it could have been.

"What did she say?" I asked.

"She said she couldn't tell what it was, but that she'd told the fire marshal everything."

My knees buckled and I leaned against the wall.

"I'm calling Mom to come get me," I said.

"After we ride," Yasmine argued. "You don't have to go where people can see you. We'll ride on the trails."

I would burst if I didn't get my pony time before there.

"Okay," I said.

Yasmine's brilliant smile split her face. We finished dressing.

"See you behind the arena." I slid my feet into my paddock boots, and shoved the door open. The door banged shut behind us.

Cricket danced when she saw me, no doubt anticipating today's ride. My heartache eased. Hanging the tack on the rack outside Cricket's stall, I opened the door to greet my mare.

CHAPTER FIVE

The short trail ride Yasmine and I took that afternoon had helped—for a time. Worry crashed back into my skull as soon as I got in Mom's car and saw how horrible she looked. Mom, who always asked how our ride was and how the horses were, hadn't said a word. Worse, she eyed me in the rearview mirror when we got into the car. She'd noticed I was upset.

We hadn't even gotten half-way home before Mom wormed out of me what Yasmine had overheard at the barn. She fumed and fretted the rest of the way. As soon as she threw the car into PARK in our driveway, she'd plucked her cellphone out of her purse and started texting someone.

Thursday was my night to get dinner out of the Crockpot and on the table. Mom cleaned up. I liked Thursdays just fine. Table set, I spooned chicken marinara onto plates and poured milk for both of us. Mom had come in the back door, passed through the kitchen, and disappeared into her office in the living room at the front of the house. She'd closed the door behind her as soon as she got inside.

I twisted the doorknob. A folder lay open on the floor, number-filled papers spilling out across the rug. Mom sat curled in the corner of the sofa, face turned to the wall. She held her cell phone to one ear, her other arm wrapped around her middle.

My mother, who never got sad, was crying. Misty trotted over and stuck her head under Mom's elbow.

"Bye," Mom said. She dropped the phone on the sofa next to her. Her hand reached down to rest on the ruff behind Misty's collar. The *whomp whomp* of the dog's furry tail against the wooden floor echoed the beat of my heart.

Tears burned in the corners of my eyes.

Mom took her hand away from the dog and put her head down on her pillowed arms. Her sobs got noisier. She never once looked my way.

I backed out of the room and pulled the door closed.

My history homework waited for me back in the kitchen. It was pathetic how grateful I was that I had to study. Concentrating was hard, but thinking about all this stuff with Mom was harder. The food got cold where it sat on the counter.

An hour later, I flipped the textbook shut and slid it to the side. My brain felt as heavy as the book itself. I was proud of myself though. After the disaster in pre-algebra, I couldn't afford to flunk the test the next day.

Misty came up behind me and pushed at my leg with her nose. The dog's tail wagged. She gave me the "I'm adorable; Feed me," look she did so well. I pushed back my chair and scratched behind her ears.

"No girl. No food," I said.

A thud shook the ceiling overhead. I looked up. My room was right over the kitchen.

"Mom?" I called out. Misty tilted her head to one side.

No answer. I shoved the chair back and went out to the stairs. Another muffled bump, followed immediately by what sounded suspiciously like a bad word. Misty and I took the stairs two at a time. I never had cleaned my room. With Mom's current state of mind, she'd probably throw half my stuff away.

The pile of dirty clothes from my floor were tossed on top of my unmade bed. Mom's back was to me, hands braced against the closet door, as if leaning on it was the only thing keeping it shut. The only thing on my floor were two empty laundry baskets. The books and stuffed animals I'd left out were nowhere to be seen. Alarm swelled in my chest.

"Mom?"

She whirled away from the closet. The door did not fly open. Her eyes narrowed. "Why haven't you cleaned this up?" she asked.

"I had history homework." I said. I'd told her in the car that I had a test the next day. But that had been before I told her what happened at the barn. My heart sank. "I was going to clean my room tonight, I swear. Where's my stuff?"

Mom put her hands on her hips.

"You've said you would clean your room for the last two weeks. It looked like a cyclone stuck it. It's a darn good thing the fire marshal—" Mom's voice cut off like lights in a thunderstorm.

The usually empty threat hung in the air between us. "Mom, I'm sorry."

"Sorry doesn't clean your room," she said, clearing her throat. Mom tossed a dirty pair of blue jeans at me. "Check the pockets."

I reached in one side and pulled out my red hoof pick that had been missing for the last two weeks. It clanked when I tossed it in the small bucket I kept by the door. There was always something that needed to go back to the barn. I checked the other pocket. Empty.

Mom plucked my "May The Horse Be With You" shirt off the bed.

I flipped the jeans onto the pile of darks in the laundry basket. Mom tossed the t-shirt on top. Two more shirts, several pairs of riding tights, and more socks than I remembered owning filled up the basket. Sorting done.

I pulled my curtain back to see if she'd put my stuff out by the curb for the trash men already. Nothing there. She hadn't taken it out yet. Still a chance to get it all back.

The light on the porch across the street caught my eye. The Danvers lived there. He owned a hardware store and he offered mom a bookkeeping job at least once a week.

"Hey," I said. "If Nelson's doesn't rebuild, you can always go work for Mr. Danvers."

Mom's eyes shifted away from my face to stare out the window. "I called him this morning."

"So when do you start?"

"He told me the job was filled. Get those clothes in the washer."

"But, Mom," I protested. "Mr. Danvers has been trying to hire you for forever."

"He's not hiring now." Mom thrust the laundry basket into my arms. "Cold. Permanent Press. Now."

I followed Mom down the stairs. My stomach was in knots. Why was that job at Danvers' Hardware gone when Mom needed it? Was this why Mom was crying?

Mom went back into the living room. The sound of the door closing behind her was loud in the silence. Tears welled at the corners of my eyes. I wasn't a baby. But I was scared. Couldn't she see that I needed her?

Stupid grown-ups. Mom always wanted a hug in front of my school friends when she dropped me off. But now, when I needed one? She went in her office and shut the door.

Misty rushed down the stairs. Her head hit the basket, which tipped laundry all down the stairs and into the hallway below. I lost my balance and sat hard on the edge on the stair tread behind me.

I waited a second or two, but Mom didn't come back out of the front room to see if I was okay. Probably thought I was sulking or something. I got up to round the clothes back up and took them out to the enclosed back porch. My fists shoved the clothes into the washer. A scoop of soap powder, and I closed the lid. Permanent Press. Cold. My fingers reached out and slapped the start button. I watched until the machine come on.

Misty barked in the hall. It was her "Demons at the door!" bark. I raced toward the sound.

Misty was in the front room by the time I got there, door closed once again with me on the wrong side of it. Hand on the doorknob, my breath whooshed out when I heard Uncle Charlie. Surely he'd notice how upset I was.

"Sit, you ball of fluff," Uncle Charlie said. Misty's barking cut off and was replaced by a satisfied yip.

"Now calm down and tell me what's going on," Uncle Charlie said.

Mom replied. I turned around and scooted up the smooth wooden stairs to the triangular step at the turn. It was far enough up that I could get up the stairs without getting caught if they came out. For once I liked that we lived in an old house. There was a small window, called a transom, over the door that allowed air to move from room to room, even when the door was closed. As I'd discovered when Mom and Dad were getting divorced, having that window open was handy. I could sit on the steps and hear everything.

"It's not over until they arrest you," Uncle Charlie said.

My heart beat so hard I was surprised Mom and Uncle Charlie couldn't hear it. *Did Uncle Charlie really think they would arrest Mom?*

There was rustling of fabric and Mom blew her nose. "Who are they going to believe, the bookkeeper in a company that is losing money left and right, or the store owner with account books to back them up?"

"You didn't do anything wrong," he said.

"Evidently that doesn't matter. The fire marshal called me this afternoon. She wants me to come in and 'talk.' The woman sounds reasonable, but I'm frightened. Nancy Everett has decided I did this, and no amount of talking to her is making any difference."

Uncle Charlie said something about fools. I was pretty sure he was talking about Mrs. Everett, but it could have been the fire marshal.

Mom's voice took on a bitter note. "Mr. Danvers believed the gossip too. Monday he offered me the same job he's been talking about for years. The fire was yesterday. Today when I called him? Position's full."

"Have you called Daniel?" I could almost see Uncle Charlie spreading large work-roughened hands as he tried to talk sense into my mother.

I sat up straighter. Dad was a lawyer, a pretty good one.

"Why would I call him? There's nothing he can do from California."

"Better he hear it from you than have someone call him to come get Sophie because you're in jail."

Come and get me?

Dad lived in California. My friends lived in Maryland. The barn was here, and even if we had to give up Cricket for a little while, Mom would get another job and we could lease her again. Moving to California would ruin everything.

Mom couldn't go to jail. She just couldn't. Besides, Mom was, well, Mom. She grounded me if I stepped out of line for anything. No way she would burn down the Nelsons' store. I clenched my hands as if to hold on to that thought. Whatever Mrs. Everett said she had on Mom could be right. There had to be a way to prove it. As much as I loved Dad, if I kept my mother out of jail, there was no question about me leaving everything behind.

Mom's voice rose and snagged my attention.

"Do you really think someone would get so embarrassed that they'd burn down a building over a hot check?"

What the heck was a "hot check?"

Mom spoke again. "The only thing I can think of is the worker we fired because Nancy said he was stealing stock. I really can't see him doing anything like this."

My spirits lifted. This thief sounded like a great suspect. Especially since he wasn't Mom or anyone else I knew.

"Did he?" Uncle Charlie asked. "Steal, I mean?" I imagined his bushy blonde eyebrows drawing together like they always did when he thought hard.

"I believed Nancy at the time. But he's a good kid. Now, with what-all she's saying about me, I know he's okay," Mom said.

"What do you mean?"

"Stock and money continued to disappear. And with this fire? It's awfully convenient that the store's insurance is way more than enough to cover the losses."

"Are you saying they burned the store down for the insurance money?" Uncle Charlie asked.

Since Mrs. Everett was out of town, "they" had to be Mr. and Mrs. Nelson. A tight knot of worry started up again in my stomach. It was easy to think about clearing Mom's name. But to do that, I had to put somebody else through in her place. The Nelson twins were pretty cute kids. Yasmine and I were their "big sisters" in Pony Club, and thinking about Mr. or Mrs. Nelson going to jail made my jaw hurt even more. It had to be the guy who got fired.

Once again, Mom's voice brought me back to the present. "Ron and Karen would never do something like this over money."

They were quiet a minute. Misty's tail started thumping again. Uncle Charlie must have started petting her.

"Not your job to find who did this. It is your job to stay out of jail. Call Daniel, get a referral," Uncle Charlie said.

"Maybe you're right," Mom replied.

Noises followed that told me they were getting up. I had better not to be caught listening. I tiptoed up to my room.

CHAPTER SIX

I got upstairs before they came out. When I opened the closet door, I expected a wave of stuff from my room to tumble out and engulf me. The closet was clean as a whistle. Where were my missing things?

"You still awake?" Mom pushed the door open. The light from the hall behind her gave her dark blonde hair a glow like one of the angels in the stained glass windows at Sunday School.

"You threw out my stuff!" I blurted.

"What? No! I boxed up some of it. Put the rest away."

Mom had packed my stuff. Acid ate at my stomach.

Shock forced the next words out of my mouth. "I don't want to move to California!"

"What are you talking about?"

"If you go to jail, then Daddy will come and get me and take me back with him." I started to cry.

She put her hands on my shoulders. "I am not going to jail."

"But you have to go talk to the fire marshal."

Mom dropped down on the bed next to me. "Children who eavesdrop can get the wrong impression. It's nothing to worry about. It's not like she's going to arrest me."

"Promise?"

"Absolutely," she said.

"So why did you pack my stuff if I'm not moving?"

"I clean when I need to do something other than worry. Or to help you when you're up to your ears in dirty laundry. That's all this was."

"I wish you'd cleaned your room rather than mine," I said.

"Sophie Marie!"

The smile on Mom's face told me she wasn't really mad.

"Want me to "draw" on your face?" Mom asked.

When I was little, Mom had done this every night to help me fall asleep. Now it was rare. I hated to admit how much I still liked it, even though I was way too big to enjoy bedtime routine with my mother.

I slid under the covers and closed my eyes.

Warm fingers smoothed softly across my cheeks and over my forehead. Erasing the little girl, she called it. Then she drew an animal's features in place of the girl's, murmuring what she drew out loud.

"Big liquid eyes," she said, passing the pads of her forefingers around my eye.

"Ears to flick back and forth." Her hands tugged a little at the tops of my ears and traced upright triangles in my hair on the sides of my head.

"And a big mouth to take apples with." She traced around my mouth and all the way out to my ears.

I opened my eyes.

"A horse, of course!" I said.

We both laughed. A serious expression chased away Mom's laughter.

Mine died too. "You won't go to jail for something you didn't do, right?" I asked.

She bent down to kiss my forehead.

"It won't happen." Saying that out loud seemed to calm her down as much as it did me.

"You going to call Daddy?" I asked.

The pinchy lines around her eyes eased.

"If I need to. But don't you worry about that. Uncle Charlie's here. And your friend Kilby's mom is also a bookkeeper. She's helped me before with the computer program we use at the shop. I'm sure she'll help me again. Sleep tight, and don't let the bedbugs bite!"

I laughed again. Mom switched on the constellation nightlight that I hadn't used in quite a while. Together we watched as the stars came out on my ceiling.

"Love you, Mom," I said.

"Love you too, Sophie-bug," she said.

Her phone rang as the door snicked shut behind her. Muted phone button tones sounded outside the door. "Caroline, thanks for returning my call," I heard her say before she moved too far away for me to hear.

Caroline was Kilby's mom.

I pulled the sheet up under my chin and gazed up at the Big Dipper over my bed.

She had help. Everything would be okay.

It had to be.

My phone buzzed under my hand. I rolled over and glared at the screen. Only Kilby would want to talk at three in the morning.

"What?" I grumbled.

"So, your mom and my mom have been talking for like, hours."

I was instantly awake.

"Mom said the books were cooked." Kilby said.

An image of limp, damp computer pages swam into my mind.

"Wait," I interrupted her. "What does that even mean?" Kilby launched into a boring recital of a lot of math facts. No way I could ever understand her.

"What does all this have to do with my mom?"

"There were two sets of books."

"Huh?" I said, feeling even stupider than before. I rubbed my jaw. It felt like it did the year before, when my dentist told my parents that I ground my teeth because of stress. Divorce will do that to a kid.

"There were two sets of store financial records. Mom said that was illegal," Kilby said.

The floorboard creaked in the hall. Mom. I thumbed the call off and rolled over on the phone so the light wouldn't show. My door opened. I flicked the *No Sound* switch on the phone and it vibrated under my stomach. Kilby, calling back.

Mom stood there for what felt like a year or two before she shut the door.

I put a couple of stuffed animals in the middle of my bed and flipped the covers over them. Pretty lame. Hopefully Mom wouldn't check on me again.

I opened the closet door and slipped inside.

I called Kilby back.

"Why would Mom keep two sets of books?" I asked.

"The real set of books was on your Mom's computer. Unfortunately, her computer is toast. There was a printout of a second set of records. The fire people found enough shreds of them left after the fire to cause trouble for your mom. They make it look like she stole from the shop. Your Mom said she didn't know anything about those numbers, but the fire marshal has some pretty big questions."

"But she wouldn't steal," I said. "There's a guy they fired for stealing a little while back," I said. "I've been thinking he might have set the fires."

"If he's even still here," Kilby said.

My mind raced. How would I find out who this guy was and if he had stuck around?

Kilby started to talk some more, this time about school, but I cut her off.

"I gotta check on something," I said.

"I'll see you tomorrow in school," Kilby said as I ended the call.

I dialed Yasmine.

"Hello?" she said. I could hear her reach over to check her Minnie Mouse alarm clock.

"Kilby called."

"Kilby felt like talking to someone in the middle of the night too?" Yasmine said.

"No, she actually had something to tell me," I said.

Yasmine started laughing.

"Wait. No. I mean..." Giggles took me. Justine had bet us once that Kilby could talk straight through lunch without anybody else saying a darned thing. I'd lost a dollar on that one. It wasn't hard to imagine Kilby calling just to talk no matter what time it was.

I gasped a little and got the laughter back under control. I felt better.

"Seriously," I said.

"Okay, shoot." Yasmine still snickered, but I knew she'd stop when she heard.

"Kilby said there were two sets of books. One that showed the store lost money. One that showed they made money."

"Your mom could be in a lot of trouble for that," Yasmine said.

"Mom didn't make the second set of books. The fire marshal evidently found them in the store after it burned. And there's more." I told her about the employee they'd fired for stealing. Then I said, "Do you know who it was?"

Yasmine sucked in a big breath. "Wish I did. That would sure make it easy."

We were quiet for a minute, thinking about easy.

"Well, I don't know," I finally said. "But if I can't find this guy and pin it on him, Mom said that the store was insured big time. What if the Nelsons burned it down for the money?" The image of the Nelson twins flashed into my mind. I couldn't imagine how they would feel if their parents had done something like that.

"It's gotta be somebody we don't even know." Yasmine had to be thinking the same thing I was.

"Agreed," I said, although I wasn't sure at all. What would we do if it turned out to be someone we knew?

"Your mom needs a lawyer," said Yasmine, yanking me back to reality.

"Dad's still got lawyer friends here. If she needs help, he can find someone." I said. After a deep breath, I told her the worst part. "If Mom goes to jail, Dad will come get me. Like, take me back with him—to live."

"We just got to be best friends, you are not moving to California," Yasmine said firmly, like saying it that way would make it true. "Besides, it'll be like what Gordon and Stan do on the *Vampire Alley* TV detective show. They always find the person who broke the rules. Guilty people aren't that smart."

Back in bed after the call, I wondered about what Yasmine had said. Book-keeping was hard. If the guilty person could do two sets then they wouldn't be as dumb as a TV villain.

The late night conversations with Kilby and Yasmine made it impossible for me to sleep. By the time my alarm buzzed the next morning, I was glad to drag myself out of bed.

I hesitated by the door to my room. I plucked the hoofpick out of the bucket and ran my finger over the cool metal. I didn't really want to show up for my lesson that afternoon. Mrs. Everett had told too many people that Mom was guilty. The trail ride Yasmine had talked me into was one thing. Lessons were in the big arena. In the middle of everything where I couldn't hide if somebody said ugly things.

Harder still to investigate if I stayed home. *Remember California.* I slipped the lost-but-now-found hoof pick into my barn bag and hefted it on my shoulder.

The aroma of blueberry pancakes greeted me outside my bedroom door. I clattered down the stairs. Mom hadn't made pancakes for forever.

Misty's nails skittered on the linoleum floor when she heard my barn bag land next to my backpack. She couldn't decide which was more exciting, me showing up, or the possibility that Mom would drop a pancake on the floor.

A steaming plate of goodness waited for me at my place. I slid into my seat and tucked my napkin into my lap.

"What's the special occasion?"

Misty's panting tongue edged closer to my plate.

I glared at the dog. She didn't budge. I pulled the pancakes back away from the edge of the table.

Mom flipped more pancakes onto a plate, steam curling from their golden-brown surfaces. "I miss being able to do things like this. While I'm home, I might as well have some fun."

"You can have all the fun you want if it includes waffles!"

Mom sat down and placed the plate on the table. I drowned mine in syrup. Pushing the bottle Mom's direction, I shoved a large bite into my mouth.

My eyes fluttered shut. More bliss-filled bites followed. Misty crawled under the table and nudged my ankle with her nose, just in case I decided to share.

Mom seemed more her old self again, "Umming" right along with me.

After I swallowed the last of my pancakes, I sprawled back in my chair. The food coma lasted for a couple of minutes, then I saw the folder on the kitchen counter with the shop accounting sheets in it. The big mess that was my life hit me full force.

Might as well just go for it. "Mom, who was that guy who stole from the shop a while back?"

"Look, you leave this alone." Mom always saw right through me.

"Is he dangerous?"

"What? No. He was just a kid. He's doing well in his new job and doesn't need you bugging him about the past."

"Do I know him?"

"You'd better get going." Mom pointed at the kitchen clock.

Yikes! I got up and dumped my plate and silverware in the dishwasher.

Mom had a damp cloth in one hand, and wiped the stove top with it. When I said, "Mom?" she turned toward me.

I hugged her like I never would get a chance to do it again.

She put her arms around me and hugged me back. Mom released a shuddering breath before I let her go.

"It's going to be okay, Mom," I said. "If the fire marshal gets grumpy, you can tell her we cleaned my room."

Mom's lips twitched upward. "I'm sure that'll do the trick." Her face lost the smile. Lines fell from her nose down past the corners of her lips and she had dark smudges under her eyes.

"It is going to be fine." Hard to believe Mom when her voice wavered that way, but it had to be true.

I gave her one last squeeze. Little did she know it was a promise that she wasn't going to jail for something she didn't do. I would find out who set that fire no matter what I had to do.

The squeal of the bus's brakes sounded out on the road. I grabbed my stuff and flew out of the house.

CHAPTER SEVEN

I yawned my way through first period before I realized something. Kids still whispered, they just didn't stare at me when they did it.

Evidently the eighth-grade boy who broke his leg in gym—and bled all over Mr. Boyd's prized wooden basketball court—was more interesting than me. The history test didn't eat my lunch. Good news, because I was plenty depressed about the barely passing grade I'd made on the pre-algebra quiz. Tanner didn't cross my path and I didn't try too hard to find him to apologize.

Just as well. I had enough on my plate worrying about Mom's visit to the fire marshall's office and my friends' lunchtime pep talk about how there was no way I would have to move to California. I nearly left the table when Justine said that her mom told her she couldn't eat lunch with me anymore if Mom went to jail. While Justine didn't say so, I got the feeling her mom felt I might as well move to California.

After the final bell of the school day, I checked my phone one more time. No text from Mom. I closed my eyes and hoped like fire that everything was okay. I quick grabbed my homework stuff out of my locker and sprinted to meet Yasmine at the car pickup area outside the gym. Mrs. Sengupta was waiting, so we climbed into the van and headed out to the barn.

Yasmine and I took a silly selfie for Mom and I hit SEND before I realized that she might still be at the fire station. Was it awful that I'd been laughing with Yasmine while she might be in trouble? I rolled down the window and let the air whip my hair around until the urge to scream was gone.

When we got to the barn, we hopped out of the van. Yasmine slammed the door behind us.

"Tanner must have been sick," Yasmine said. "He didn't come to school today."

At least I didn't have to make excuses for not apologizing yet. "I bet he talked his mom into letting him come ride, even if he did skip school."

"I hope so."

Yasmine looked all over, but she couldn't find Tanner. I knew I had to talk to him sometime, but I was still relieved.

I would apologize. For one thing, Mom and Dad had taught me to be polite. For another, Tanner was my friend, even if his mom was being mean.

Cricket was really well-groomed by the time I got the nerve up to take her out of the stall and go to the arena for my lesson. Cricket and I left the barn at the exact same time a strange woman came out of the arena on Vee. She rode up to Mrs. Everett, who stood at the arena gate, right between me and my lesson. The woman hopped off, flashed a big smile, handed off the reins, and then shook Mrs. Everett's free hand. Who was this woman and why was she riding Vee?

Mrs. Everett strode in my direction and my brain went into overdrive trying to figure out how I could hide from her while I was leading a fifteen-hand horse. I was still shaking when she passed us like we weren't there.

She stopped where Luis and another groom stood by the barn. The second groom held a lead rope for a grazing horse. Mrs. Everett handed the reins to the him, despite the fact that Luis was right there.

"Make sure he's clean and dry before you put him up. Her clear voice carried to where I cowered on the far side of my pony. " she said. "The vet is on her way to do the pre-purchase exam."

The woman was a buyer. And it sounded like they'd sold him already. No wonder Tanner was sick.

The groom shrugged at Luis, but with Mrs. Everett watching, he handed the grazing horse's lead rope to Luis and took Vee from Mrs. Everett. What was with her? Did she hate everyone now?

Yasmine came up beside me, Bourbon at her side "She really is going to sell Tanner's horse!"

I looked out at the arena. Some of the riders stared at me, and I could almost hear them thinking, "She's the daughter of that woman. You know. Jaimie Allen, who burned down the tack shop."

I turned Cricket back toward the barn. I couldn't deal with this.

"You are not leaving." Yasmine saw right through me. "You know how much better you felt when you rode yesterday. No one will pick on you in front of Queenie."

That much was probably true. But that didn't make this easy.

I put my foot in the stirrup and tried to swing onto Cricket's back.

The saddle slipped to one side. I'd been so worried about what was going on around me that I'd forgotten to check my girth. That was just plain stupid.

Yasmine got on Bourbon. Laughing, she said, "Forget something?"

"I know. Stupid me." My face flushed as I said it.

"Hey, don't sweat it," my friend said. "C'mon."

She went into the arena while I put the saddle back on top of the horse and did the girth up right. Then I went around and rechecked everything else, just in case. *Good to go.* I swung up on Cricket and joined Yasmine in the arena.

Brandon and Brigitte had the lesson before us. It was the first time I'd seen them since the fire, but they headed straight for Yasmine and me like they always did. Raven and Star, their two adorable black ponies, nosed Cricket and Bourbon while the kids chattered about their lesson. I looked around for their mom and spotted Mrs. Nelson in a lawn chair by the side of the arena. Her right arm was in a sling. The burn she'd gotten must have been bad.

Cricket tossed her head as my body tightened up. Mrs. Nelson was so nice. How would she feel about me now? If Mrs. Everett blamed Mom and glared at me, would the twins' parents feel the same way she did? Yasmine and I stayed with the twins every Friday night while the Nelsons went out to dinner. What if they didn't want me babysitting anymore?

"Those ponies won't cool themselves out, you know," Queenie called. "Let your reins out so they can stretch and let them walk." When Queenie used that tone, everyone obeyed. The twins and their ponies took a long rein and walked away.

Mrs. Nelson stood up and headed our way. Two of the gossipy women over by the barn stopped talking and watched like rubberneckers on the freeway.

Cricket backed up a step or two. I'd tensed up and pulled on the reins. I let go and she stood still.

Mrs. Nelson had a big smile on her face just like usual. Cricket shook her head from side to side like a dog shedding water. I'd clenched my hands again. Even with the smile, she might still blame Mom like Mrs. Everett did.

"I've called your mom a million times today," Mrs. Nelson said. "Is she here?"

The flutter in my stomach seemed to have moved into my throat. I tried to answer, but no words came out.

Yasmine spoke up. "Pretty sure she'll be here later."

"Yasmine! Sophie!" the twins cried as they rode by. "Can you bring your Pony Pal books again? It's Friday!"

"Stop that, you two," Mrs. Nelson said. She turned to me. "No date night this week, what with all the excitement. I hope you and Yasmine can come by this weekend and give the twins their fix."

Mrs. Nelson leaned closer, her eyes intent on my face. She spoke so that no one else could hear. "Your mom's going to be okay. Remember that." She patted my leg and turned to go back to her chair under the maple tree, all the world as if she didn't know what Mrs. Everett said about Mom and the fire. A flare of hope exploded in my chest.

Queenie finished up with the twins and they left the arena, chattering as usual.

"You two ladies ready?" Queenie asked. "Tanner's out today." She cut her eyes toward the barn. "He should be here next time."

Yasmine and I nodded.

Because we'd jumped Tuesday, Fridays were flatwork. Between the fact that Yasmine liked this kind of riding a whole lot more than I did, and wondering what Mrs. Nelson knew that I didn't, I didn't really pay attention like I should have.

Queenie yelled my name.

I pulled up short at the tone in her voice. A rider cantered by and took the jump in front of us. The woman yelled back at me after they landed.

"Sorry," I called after her.

Queenie tore off her Oriole's cap and threw it in the sand on her way over, a sure sign that I was really in trouble.

"Sophie Marie Allen!"

Boy did she sound like my mother.

"I know. That was really stupid."

Queenie lowered her voice. "Look, I know you've got a lot on your mind right now, but you have got to pay attention when you're on a horse. There are other people in this ring. Someone might get hurt."

"Yes, Ma'am," I said.

"Now go do that serpentine again," Queenie said. She stooped down to pick up her baseball cap, "and do it like you've been taught, not like you're following a will-o'-the-wisp."

I felt a smile tug at my lips. "Yes, Ma'am," I said again.

And I did. Best serpentine I've ever done.

Best of all, Queenie said I could post all the tack-cleaning fliers I wanted and she'd tell everyone I did a great job.

I still felt pretty good when I got back to Cricket's stall. I had almost finished with my after-the-ride grooming routine on my mare when Tanner entered the barn and walked my way. Yasmine peered around the corner behind him and made encouraging motions with her hands. I rolled my eyes.

Tanner got to Cricket's stall and stepped inside. He looked out in the aisle, up at the ceiling, and then down at his toes.

"Hey," I said. "You okay?"

"Sure," Tanner said. "Ducky. Mom let me stay home from school so I could be with Vee before the new owners came to pick him up."

"I'm glad you could be with him."

"Yeah." Tanner stuck his hands in his pockets and looked down. A silence fell.

I opened my mouth, but nothing came out. I'd been an idiot, but if I said that out loud, I would sound even more stupid.

Yasmine bounced up and down on the balls of her feet at the end of the aisle, hands on hips. She was trying to read our lips from fifty feet away. I sighed. Better get it over with.

"I'm sorry for yesterday at school," I said.

"Yeah," he said.

I waited for him to say something else. The longer the silence stretched, the more my stomach hurt.

He turned away from an apparently fascinating cobweb on the beam outside Cricket's stall and met my gaze. "You've had a rough couple of days."

"You too. I'm *really* sorry about Vee."

"Yeah," Tanner said. "It kind of stinks."

"At least he won't try to kill you anymore," I said.

Tanner choked. "Yeah, that's a good thing." Then his eyes shifted a little to the left and a hiccup shook him.

"We can still be friends, right? Even if our moms aren't?"

"Yeah."

He flashed me a small grin. His hand came up in a little wave as he walked away.

I meant it about being friends. Kids had to be on our own parents' side. But that didn't mean that I didn't still think Tanner was pretty cool for liking horses—and my best-friend. Evidently he felt the same way.

Luis walked up and tugged the stall door open across the aisle. He put the wheelbarrow in front of the door, and went in to clean the stall. He chucked dirty shavings and manure into the wheelbarrow. Devil, Queenie's grey thoroughbred gelding, gently nudged Luis in the side with his nose. One of the older teenage riders from the competition barn shot down the aisle and into Devil's stall. She never looked my way. The girl was a competitive rider, one who'd recently shot up on the leader board. To her, people like me were invisible.

"Did you hear the latest about the fire?" she demanded of Luis.

"Look, that's all old news," Luis said, bending over to pick up a muckrake full of soiled bedding that smelled strongly of ammonia. He tossed it outside the stall into the waiting wheelbarrow.

"They were about to file bankruptcy!" the girl said. "You used to work there. Did you know they were having trouble?"

Luis shushed her and waved his hand in my direction. So much for invisible. Mrs. Nelson could promise Mom would be fine all she wanted. People still talked trash about her. I was not fine with that.

The nosey rider turned her face toward us, plastered a fake smile on her nasty face, and took off fast.

Luis tossed a last forkful of smelly shavings into the wheelbarrow and pushed it out of the way so he could close Devil's stall door. He came over to our side of the aisle.

"Shake it off. No way your mom would set a fire like this." Luis gave Tanner a cool glance as he said this.

"How do you know?" Not what I meant to say. Everyone said Mom would be fine. No one knew that, though; not until whoever set that fire got caught.

Luis smiled. "I stocked shelves for Nelsons' for awhile. Your mom was really nice to me, even when Mrs. Everett accused me of some bad stuff. Mrs. Allen's a good lady."

He came out, closed the stall, and wheeled the muck-filled wheelbarrow out toward the manure spreader behind the barn.

I stared after him.

Unlike my ex-friend Ingrid, I was good at math. Luis had worked at the shop. Mrs. Everett accused him of bad stuff. He had to be the store thief.

There went my crush.

CHAPTER EIGHT

A half-hour later, Yasmine and I stood at the corner of the barn by the parking lot. No one was around but us.

"Mom won't be here for another fifteen minutes," I said. "I'm going to go look and see if there is anything in Luis's car to start a fire."

"Are you crazy? We're twelve years old. We'll be in a mess of trouble if we poke our noses where they don't belong!"

"California, Yasmine."

My friend was silent. She didn't want me to move any more than I did.

"Stay here." I pointed at the corner of the barn. "Make sure I know if someone comes."

Yasmine leaned against the faded red boards.

I walked toward the small group of cars parked at the far end of the area. That was where the grooms all parked. Luis drove a dark blue car. There were three dark blue cars and two light blue ones. Was there a law somewhere that said all grooms had to drive the same color car?

I closed my eyes and thought back to the last time I'd seen him drive off. One of the tail lights was smashed. Sure enough, only one of the cars had a broken tail light. I looked around. No one there. I pulled on the driver side door. Locked. Swallowing disappointment, I moved around to the passenger side door.

It eased open. The overwhelming smell of smoke wrinkled my nose. Good thing I didn't like him anymore. Smoking was disgusting. I looked back toward Yasmine. She glared at me. I turned back to the car.

I flipped open the glove compartment. Receipts and gum wrappers spilled everywhere. They crinkled under my fingers as I stuffed them back in the small opening. I shoved the door shut and heard the catch click. A red plastic lighter caught my eye in the center console, next to an empty pack of Marlboros. I picked it up. You could start a fire with a lighter. But did it count as evidence?

"Hey, Luis," Yasmine said in a loud voice.

"What's up, little girl?" Luis answered. His footfalls didn't stop.

I slid out over the cracked plastic seat. I didn't dare slam the door. I pressed it shut, but it didn't close all the way. No time to do anything about that.

The next car over was easy enough to get behind. I popped my head up in time to see Luis headed my way. I ducked down as fast as I could. Had he seen me? I still had the lighter in my hand. It felt like a bomb. I stuffed it in my jeans pocket.

"Sophie?" Yasmine called. "Did you find your hair clip?"

Smart. I undid my hair and stood up with the clip in my hand. "Found it!"

I nodded at Luis as I walked by. He smiled back.

Mom pulled into the parking area seconds after Luis had nearly caught me red-handed.

Yasmine and I climbed into the back seat of the car.

"Can Yasmine spend the night?" I asked Mom.

Mom's face went blank. "Not going to sit for the twins tonight?" she said in a too-bright tone.

"Mrs. Nelson said her arm hurt too much to go to a restaurant. They want us to come over tomorrow instead."

Mom's face softened. She looked at the two of us hopeful girls and shrugged.

"Why not," she said. "We'll go to Yasmine's. She can pick up what she needs if her mom says it's okay to stay over."

Once we got our seat belts on, Mom looked over her shoulder and backed out of the parking space.

Luis had already pulled out and was at the end of the lane. As he turned left onto the road, the passenger door flew open. I should have known not being able to close that door would be trouble.

I reached out and grabbed Yasmine's arm. I pointed.

"I couldn't shut the door all the way," I whispered. Yasmine's eyes grew wide.

Mom finished backing up and shifted gears.

Luis pulled over to the side of the road. He went around the car and ran his hand down the edge of the car door. He stared at it for a minute, then reached down to pick something up inside the car. He glanced back at the barn, but there was no way to see his expression from where we sat.

Mom hit the brakes hard, yanking our attention away from Luis.

Mrs. Nelson's face appeared in the window next to mine. She waved, then tapped on Mom's window. I waved back, then looked for Luis's car. Gone.

"Jaimie?" Mrs Nelson said to Mom.

My fingernails scraped against the cloth seat as my fist balled up. Even though she'd been nice to me earlier, she might be different with Mom.

Mom looked back at me in the rear-view mirror. Her lips were white. When Mrs. Nelson repeated Mom's name, she finally rolled down her window.

"You don't have to avoid me, you know," Mrs. Nelson said.

"How's your hand?" Mom asked.

Mrs. Nelson wiggled the hand in the sling. Her nose scrunched up as if that hurt more than she'd expected.

"I've been calling you, but you haven't picked up." Mrs. Nelson looked more puzzled than upset.

I watched Mom. I couldn't see her whole face, but enough to know how she felt. Mrs. Nelson was herself. That meant a lot.

"Don and I know better than to believe all the crazy things his sister's saying," Mrs. Nelson said.

I knew I liked this woman.

The thin lines around Mom's mouth eased. "Thank you for saying that. It means a lot."

Mrs. Nelson put her unbandaged hand on Mom's arm. "See you tomorrow when Sophie and Yasmine can come stay with the twins," she said."

Mom looked over her shoulder at us. We nodded back.

"Call and let us know what time you want them over there," Mom said. "And thanks. You and Don mean a lot to me."

"You too, Jamie." Mrs. Nelson went back inside the barn.

Mom drove away.

When we pulled into the Sengupta's driveway, Yasmine and I dashed inside to ask her mom if she could stay over. Unfortunately, if we weren't going to be at the Nelsons', Mrs. Sengupta wanted Yasmine to babysit her little brother. I was bummed. To make up for it, Mom stopped for dinner on the way home.

We sat in the front room. An hour later, an empty pizza box abandoned on the coffee table in front of us. Mom and I each curled up in our own corner of the living room sofa. One of my old kid movies played on the TV. Somehow, watching a princess flitter across the screen didn't distract me the way I thought it would. Maybe if she had a horse.

I slid a hand in my pocket. It closed around the lighter. I'd tried to ask Mom about the shop thief, but that was before I knew it was Luis. Second time might be the charm.

"How mad was Luis when Nelson's fired him? Mad enough to start that fire?" I asked.

Mom sat up. "I told you to let that alone. Luis didn't steal anything, and he's doing a great job for Queenie. Accusing him of another crime he didn't commit isn't right," Mom said.

"They're accusing you. And that's exactly why we need to find out who it really was."

"Wait just a minute, young lady. *We* don't need to 'find out' anything. The fire marshal has things under control." Mom waved her hand at the television. "Watch your favorite movie, will ya?"

The movie hadn't been my favorite for years. I didn't care if we missed the whole thing. "We can't just ignore this."

Mom narrowed her eyes at me. "No one is ignoring this. So far Nancy Everett is the only one who thinks I had anything to do with this. You don't need to be too worried about her."

My feet hit the floor as I sat up straight. "Uncle Charlie said you needed a lawyer."

"When did he tell you that?" Mom asked.

One hand crept up so I could bite a nail.

"I'm going to kill Charlie." Mom sighed.

I yelped as I bit my tongue.

"I forgot. Eavesdropping again." An irritated look skittered across Mom's face. Mom reached over and flicked the finger out of my mouth. "Stop biting your nails," she said. "And to answer your question, Uncle Charlie's right, but it's not because I had anything to do with the fire."

"What did the fire marshal say?" I finally asked the question I'd been thinking about all evening.

"It was routine. They have to check with all of the employees is all."

She didn't look at me when she said that, so I didn't know if I believed her. I waited. She pressed her lips together and turned away. She wasn't going to tell me.

"I think I'll go to bed now." I wanted to talk to Yasmine.

"Don't you want to finish the movie?"

I looked at the screen. The heroine was singing about finding love.

"Not feeling very Disney," I said.

"Let the dog out." Mom stayed put, face turned toward the television as if she was truly interested in the movie.

Misty and I walked to the back door. The night air chilled my bare arms as I let her out. Couldn't even tell it was spring by the weather. Rubbing my arms with my hands didn't do a thing.

Metal clanked on metal out by the shed.

"Misty! Leave those trash cans alone. Inside." My voice rose on the last word as a shadow shifted by the garage door. Raccoons. The last time Misty had nearly killed one. I shivered. It had been really gross.

I had to call her a second time before the dog came. Out on the street in front of the house, a truck engine roared to life as I tugged the door shut behind us. Misty's sleek fur brushed my hand as she went past me into the warmth on the kitchen. I stopped by the front room to give Mom another hug before heading to bed.

Upstairs I peeled off my clothes and started a new pile by the dresser. The jeans thunked when they hit the floor. I stepped over and picked the jeans back up. My fingers closed around the plastic lighter. Where to hide it? If Mom found the lighter, I'd be grounded for life.

My secret room was just the place. I pulled open my closet door. I shoved the hangers off to one side and rocked back, urgency stopped cold by the neatly organized shelves in front of me. The Nate the Great books were gone, as were half my stuffed animals. My chest rose and fell as I huffed a protest. I touched the spine of the first Boxcar Children book, then *A Horse Named Dog*. My favorites were still there. My Pony Club manuals and horse-related reference books were on my desk, so they were safe too.

I turned to go down and demand my things back. The hard plastic lighter in my hand stopped me. I turned back to the practically empty shelves. Dad had built these when I was little. They were great for two reasons: storage for me——and because I'd been afraid of the monster I was convinced lived in the crawl space behind my closet. The bell on the shelves would warn me if something came and tried to get me. "No bell, no monster," Dad had told me.

The bell had never rung. Eventually I'd stopped being scared of the crawl space and realized it was the perfect hiding place for a girl who didn't want to be found. I reached up and felt along the top of the shelves. Fingers touched the hook on the left side of the bookcase, right behind my copy of *The Girl Who Remembered Horses*. I flipped the catch, moved one hand to clasp the bell, and tugged the bookshelf toward me. It swung open with a tiny rasp as it scraped against the floor.

Stale air blew past me as I stooped to fit through the opening. My hand waved around in front of me and snagged the light cord. One tug and the bare light bulb switched on.

My secret room was much as I remembered it, except for five cardboard boxes to the left of the doorway. A black marker labeled them. "Books." "Stuffed Animals."

Relief filled me. My stuff was safe. The swinging light from the bulb washed over the boxes and my old toys. The dust on the floor was smudged from Mom's footsteps.

I couldn't just put the lighter down and trust that she wouldn't find it. With my luck, Mom would decide tomorrow was a good time to go through the boxed stuff. The light hit my old rocking horse, Chester. The hiding place of all hiding places. When I was six and way too big to be on the horse, I rocked a little too enthusiastically, imagining Chester and I led the field at the local hunt. We'd fallen over hard enough to crack the side of the plastic pony where the painted-on saddle bags pooched out. Now the saddle bag lifted enough to get a hand inside the horse. I scooted over and plunged my hand in. It met the hard corner of my old diary. Still safe and sound. I shoved the lighter down under my diaries.

"Sophie?" Mom's voice said outside my door.

The secret room door snicked shut as Mom stuck her head in my bedroom. I grabbed my sleep t-shirt and stepped out of the closet.

"It's cold in here." Mom frowned.

"Is it?" It was. The temperature had really dropped from all that cold air in my secret room. "I left my window open when I was downstairs."

"We can't afford to heat the entire Eastern Shore."

I'd heard that one before.

"Yes, ma'am."

"Sleep tight."

"You too, Mom."

She left. The lighter would be okay where it was. If Mom decided to read my diaries, then the lighter would just be one more thing for her to be mad at me about.

I was snuggled up under the covers, Misty spread over half the bed, when I heard Mom come up and go into her room. My unanswered questions about Luis and what the fire marshal had said haunted me. I rolled over and snuggled against the dog.

CHAPTER NINE

Most kids slept late on Saturday morning. Not me. It was my favorite day of the week. For one thing, I had Cricket all day. Almost as good, our Pony Club unmounted meeting was every Saturday morning where we got to learn all kinds of cool stuff about horses. Queenie had an equine dentist coming that morning to talk about teeth and bits.

I sat on the end of my bed. One hand stroked Misty's back where she lay next to me, her muzzle warm against my thigh. The dog's tail gave a steady beat of happiness against the quilt. The sun winked in my window. Time to get dressed.

Looking around, my mood soured. First the fire business and then Mom messing with my room. Nothing was where it was supposed to be. I finally found my zebra-stripped socks in my dresser. We'd had a great horse management judge at rally one time who wore crazy socks. I decided I would wear them too. The little kids loved it. Finding my Pony Club polo, riding tights, and belt took longer. For some reason Mom had hung them up in my closet. Not where they belonged.

Dressed, I headed outside to start my weekend chores. First up, empty the trash. Misty ran ahead of me to the garage. One of the trash cans lay on its side. Stupid raccoons. I righted it, and pulled the lid off. Even though I'd seen the boxes up in my secret room, I had to check. Mom might have thrown away something important. I was sure glad none of my stuff was in them. The smell was horrible.

Can to the curb, I ran back inside and did my inside chores. Then I double checked to make sure I had more tack-cleaning fliers in my barn bag. That finished, I went into the kitchen and poured a big glass of milk and a bowl of cereal. Misty parked herself at my feet and tried to look like she was starving. As if. I'd fed her myself.

Mom came in. "That looks good," she said. She grabbed a bowl of cereal and poured milk on top. She leaned against the counter and took a spoonful.

I didn't ask Mom about Luis again, or the papers she'd put inside Chester. It wouldn't do me any good.

In no time at all we were both done. Mom got up and switched on the water to rinse her bowl. I had a lot to find out at the barn, and I needed a plan. I would have fun, but I needed to dig around some too.

The porch door slammed shut behind me. I'd think better outside. I propped my barn bag on the steps as Misty ran past me. She ran up with her ball. I threw it.

Find evidence Luis set the fire.

The dog dropped the ball at my feet. I tossed it, thinking about the lighter I'd taken from Luis's car and how hard it would be to start a big fire with it. Then I thought about how nice he'd been to me and the other girls, even though you could tell Luis didn't want all the attention we gave him.

Might not be Luis. But if not Luis, then who set that fire?

I leaned against the siding by the steps and patted Misty's head when she came back and dropped the ball.

I hadn't seen inside Luis's trunk.

Mom came out and rattled her keys at me.

"One last time," I said to the dog. I tossed the ball. Misty tore after it.

Mom dropped me at the barn.

"You staying?" She did sometimes.

"Not today. Mrs. Nelson called and asked me to run a couple of errands for her while her arm is out of commission."

Good. Mom wouldn't be there to tell me to stop looking into Luis.

I met Yasmine in the barn aisle after I gave Cricket her treat.

"Got some more things to check out," I told my friend.

"Stay out of Luis's car," Yasmine warned.

"Yeah, yeah." I waved my fliers at her.

Yasmine went off to the tack room to gather our teaching supplies. She obviously thought I had agreed.

The parking area was busy. I hung out by the barn door. With the Pony Club meeting starting soon, everyone cleared the area fast. Yasmine would be mad when I wasn't on time, but she'd cover for me until I could get there.

I posted my fliers in the tack rooms and the bathroom. That done, I walked outside and checked the passenger side of Luis's car. Locked. Guess having the door fly open had spooked him.

I looked over at the driver's door. The lock was up. I walked around and opened the door. The smoke stink blasted my nose. My throat tightened. I coughed to clear it and bent down.

My finger hooked the trunk release. The trunk popped open. I went and looked inside. He had a ton of dirty tack in there. Maybe he wasn't stupid enough to keep evidence in his car.

Hang on.

There were a bunch of rags in the corner of the trunk. I leaned over and snagged one.

"Find what you were looking for?" Luis asked.

I jumped three feet straight up off the ground like Cricket did on the trails when she smelled a deer.

"Your trunk was open," I said. Not exactly a lie.

"I knew someone messed with my car yesterday. Not cool, little girl." My heart beat so hard I swear I could hear it knocking against my chest.

Luis grabbed my arm with one hand while he whipped the dirty towel away with his other. He tossed the rag back in the trunk and slammed it shut.

"What's going on here?" Tanner's face swam into view over Luis's shoulder.

Luis let go of my arm. "She broke into my car."

As the barn hand stepped away from me, my breathing eased up.

Luis took another step back. "Stay away from my stuff."

It felt like a threat.

Tanner waited until Luis was gone. "Seriously, what are you thinking?"

"Yasmine's a snitch," I said.

"You'd better be glad she sent me out here. Did he hurt you?"

"Just scared me," I admitted.

"You can't go breaking into someone's car and not expect them to be angry."

I didn't answer. I was busy sniffing the hand that had held the rag from Luis's trunk.

Yasmine came around the corner.

"Hope you found her before she did something stupid," Yasmine said.

"After," Tanner said.

"Right here," I said.

"Tough," they said together.

I glared at them. It hurt that they teamed up on me. Neither of them understood .

I stuck my hand out. "I found some rags in his trunk. My hand smells like gasoline now."

Yasmine took a cautious whiff. "Smells like hoof oil to me," she said.

"Really?" I said. "I thought it smelled like gasoline."

"Would you stop this?" Yasmine said. "I told you. We're twelve. Let the adults figure this out."

"You'd leave it alone if you were smart. You might not like what you find," Tanner said.

"Did you really just say that out loud?" I couldn't believe it.

"Stop it, Sophie. You're fighting the wrong person." Yasmine took a step closer to Tanner.

"His mom is running around telling everyone my mother burned down the tack shop. Now he's doing it too." I took a step closer to Yasmine and glared at her. "Should I just let Mom go to jail? I guess now you have a boyfriend you don't care if I have to move."

"That's not true," Yasmine said.

"What do you mean move?" Tanner asked. He took a step closer.

My hands flashed out and pushed him away.

For a second everything hung in the air.

Then Yasmine's face closed. For a second she looked like she had when she shoved Ingrid away from me in school. "It's time for us to give our lesson." Her tone made it clear that it would be fine with her if I skipped out.

My wrist throbbed where Luis had gripped it. "I'm ready."

The little kids mostly paid attention while we showed them how to tell if a bit fit a horse's mouth. *"One finger on each side. Make sure it's on the bars of the mouth, not on the teeth."* Then we held up a dirty bit while saying, *"Would you put that in your mouth?"* We had them clean a bunch of Queenie's schooling bits to drive home just how gross the mouthpieces could get.

The work done, the kids homed in on the barn door, wild to go out and run wild. Yasmine took off without waiting for me. I thought about leaving, but I really wanted to hear what the equine dentist had to say. Maybe Yasmine would understand better once she'd had time to think about it.

I went over and joined the lesson. Yasmine moved away from me to stand next to Tanner. One of the older girls moved over to stand next to me. "Don't sweat about it," she whispered to me, then gave my shoulder a little bump with her fist. Her grin told me that was her way of saying she was on my side. My back straightened. Yasmine might be mad at me, but my Pony Club family was still there for me. I reached over and bumped her back.

The presentation was really cool. The dentist had skulls from different-aged horses. Lined up, they clearly showed the progression of the Galvayne's Groove on the upper corner incisor.

"It shows up on that tooth and that tooth only, in the middle of that tooth," the dentist told us, "so the groove appears at age five as the tooth grows out and then disappears after about age twenty. Horses' teeth grow throughout their lifetime."

Most people didn't understand how much real knowledge we learned in Pony Club. All they heard was the name. *Pony* makes people think of cute little fluffy animals. Horses are amazing athletes. And we learn serious stuff in our lessons.

The dentist finished up by talking about bits, repeating what we'd told the little kids about where they should lay in the mouth and how to fit them. She talked a little about how the thickness and number of breaks in the metal affected the horse and showed us examples of bits she wanted to make sure we never, ever used. One of them looked like twisted barbwire. My mouth hurt just to look at it.

After I thanked the dentist, I waited for Yasmine. She hung back to ask the speaker a couple of questions. My shoulders tightened. I left to go tack up Cricket. Yasmine and I always trail rode after our unmounted lesson. I'd go even if she didn't want to go out with me.

I had my mare saddled and ready to go by the time Yasmine showed up. She lugged her saddle over to Bourbon's stall and set it down. I stepped out of Cricket's stall.

"You still want to trail ride?" I held my breath.

"I guess so."

Yasmine didn't look at me, but she'd said yes. That counted for something.

Luis walked by and disappeared down the far end of the aisle. My heart skipped a beat, but for a very different reason today than it had the day before. He'd threatened me. It had to be because he was guilty.

As we mounted to go on our hack through the woods, Tanner came out of the barn on Vee. Not sold yet, then. My breath whooshed out when Tanner reined his horse in the opposite direction. I didn't know how I'd feel if Yasmine had invited him along.

The horses pricked their ears forward as we headed through the open gate to the bridle path. Their strides loosened up as they always did when they were happy.

Yasmine and I didn't talk much on the ride. Slowly, as it did every time I got on the horse, the outside world fell away. The slow steady cadence of Cricket's hooves against the soft forest floor comforted me. The scent of pine mixed with the previous night's rain surrounded me. The fresh air stroked my cheek when we picked up the trot.

I held a hand up to catch a branch so that it wouldn't slap me in the face as we walked through the narrowest part of the trails. I looked back. Yasmine shoved the same branch away and rode up next to me as the trail widened. She smiled. Riding had worked its magic. She wasn't angry anymore.

We arrived in the field furthest away from the barn. I leaned down and opened the gate. Both Cricket and Bourbon went through. Yasmine hopped off and closed the gate. We took the tack off the horses, hung it on the fence next to the gate and let the horses loose.

We always went to this pasture on our trail rides because of the oak tree in the center of the field. Our Pony Club had a tradition. After we'd passed our first test and earned a certification, we got to carve our initials on the tree. Then we knew we were truly a part of the club.

Mostly though, we came out there because the tree was fun to climb. Once up in the branches, it was the best place ever to sit and talk. Yasmine and I climbed up the branches. Cricket and Bourbon munched the newly greening timothy grass. I stopped to rub my initials for luck.

I settled in the crook of a branch about halfway up the tree and closed my eyes, listening to the gentle breeze ruffling the new leaves around me. We talked about school and about which horse shows we'd like to enter now that we were moving into show season. Yasmine was better at the dressage shows, but I'd always loved the feeling of freedom that I got when Cricket and I ran cross-country. No horse-eating blue barrels there! After a bit I climbed down and lay in the new orchard grass at the base of the tree and peered at the clouds as they danced across the powder blue sky overhead. Cricket came over to see what I was doing and blew in my ear. I rolled quickly away so she wouldn't slobber on me. She ate the tuft of grass where my head had been.

Way up in the tree, Yasmine was in the middle of a complicated story about how mean her older brother had been that week. Suddenly, she yelled something I couldn't understand. A second's pause, then shredded pieces of bark rained down on the top of my head. Yasmine yelled, "Look out!" as she jumped the rest of the way down.

"What's wrong?" I asked.

"Fire!" She could barely get the word out. "Can't you hear the twin's ponies? They must be in the barn." She ran across the paddock to catch Bourbon, who promptly shied away to the far side of the field.

I reached into my boot to pull my phone out and came up empty. Bad time to leave it in my backpack!

"My phone's back at the barn. What about yours?" I asked.

"No signal." Yasmine huffed as she gave up on Bourbon and caught Cricket's mane.

I grabbed Cricket's bridle and ran over to her. She let me slip it over her head. Thank goodness. We threw the saddle on and I used the fence to climb on. "Give me your phone," I urged. "I'll ride out until I get a signal."

Yasmine handed the phone to me and I stuck it in the side of my boot, turned Cricket and aimed her at the low point in the fence line that would take me to the Nelsons'. As I sailed over the top board, Bourbon danced away again from Yasmine's outreached hand.

CHAPTER TEN

We had to jump two fence lines before Cricket and I got to the Nelsons' farm. After the first one, I hauled on the reins to turn the mare into a stop. I punched in 9-1-1 again and hit dial. It didn't go through.

I lost my balance going over the second fence, but my amazing horse stayed under me so that I didn't fall.

The crackle of flames licking at the wooden barn grew louder as we got to the pasture on the hill overlooking the Nelsons' barn. Cricket skittered back sharply. I kicked my feet out of the stirrups. I swung up and over her hind end when the frightened mare began to rear. I landed on my feet, shaking. She had never, ever done that before. Cricket tore the reins out of my hand and ran to the far end of the field.

I pulled the phone out and hit redial. The heat that close to the barn was horrible.

"9-1-1. How may I direct your call?"

The operator answered!

"Fire!" I panted. "The barn is on fire." I began to cry with relief. I'd gotten through.

"Where are you?" The ponies frantic whinnies nearly drowned out the calm voice of the operator.

Between sobs, I gasped out, "Nelson Farm on Bear Branch Road."

"Are you inside the barn?"

"No," I said.

"Good. Stay away from the building. What is the address?"

"I don't know!" One of the ponies neighed, the shrill sound hurting my ears. I took a couple of steps toward the barn.

"Do you know any cross streets?"

"We turn off Route 1 to get here." The ponies' hooves beat a sharp staccato against the stall walls. I had to do something. I jogged toward the door at the end of the barn.

"Working on your phone location now," the operator said.

One of the ponies trumpeted in pain. I ran to the barn door and started to open it. The door handle vibrated under my hand. Almost as soon as I touched it, I had to let go. I stared at my blistered palm. How could the handle burn me that quickly?

"Ow!" I said as sharp pain rose. The phone squawked in my uninjured hand. I put it back to my ear.

"I burned my hand on the door. The ponies are in there!"

I had to get them out. I had to.

"Do not go into the building," the operator's voice rose. "Is anyone else there with you?"

"My friend's on her way."

"Good. I've dispatched the truck. It should be there soon."

A sharp crack sounded. The window closest to me burst outward. Shards of glass sprayed in every direction. Flames shot out the now-open window.

I jumped back and bumped into the water trough. Water sloshed down the back of my legs. Yasmine's phone slipped out of my hand and landed at the bottom of the trough. I fished the phone out and shook it.

Black screen.

I pressed the power button and put it back up to my ear.

No sound.

I used a string of bad words that would have had me grounded for a month if Mom was nearby.

I stuffed the phone down my boot. The operator said help was on the way. I hoped she was right.

I looked at the barn. Help might not get there in time to get the ponies out.

The fire was mostly around the end farthest away from the Nelsons' house. The door by the feed room might be easier to open.

The heat wasn't as harsh on this side. I wrapped my good hand in my jacket, and then reached out and touched the door panel. It didn't seem as hot as the front doors had. A chain wound through the door handles. I ripped it off with my covered hand and yanked open the door.

Good thing I'd moved to the side. Fire shot out the door. I dove away from the flames, rolled away to the side, and came up running. I rounded the corner of the building, and ran smack into somebody. We grabbed each other to keep our balance.

"Sophie," Tanner said. "Thank goodness."

"Where..."

"No time. Over here" Tanner grabbed my uninjured hand and tugged me partway down the barn wall.

"I think this part used to be a door. If we can just get these boards off..."

Tanner put his hand around the end of a plank and pulled. It bowed outward, but stayed stuck at the other end. I wrapped my good hand around one side of the board and pulled as hard as I could. It didn't move. I looked around for something to use to pry at my end and remembered an old metal fencepost close to the door I'd just opened. I scrambled up to get it.

"What are you...oh, great!" Tanner said when I returned with the T-post.

Together we wedged the post behind the board and pulled back. The stubborn end of the plank popped out. We looked inside. A horse's legs wove in and out of sight through the smoke. Two of the hind legs had socks. Brigitte's pony, Star. Brandon's Raven was solid bay.

We quickly widened the opening. Smoke rushed out. It was hot, but I couldn't see actual flames. We'd only cleared about four boards before Star realized the hole was there. She threw herself against the wall. From that point we only had to pry one end of the next plank off before she broke herself loose.

As she thundered by, the other pony, Raven, whinnied his distress from the stall next to Star's.

Tanner plunged through the narrow opening. I started to follow him, but a beam cracked overhead and sparks showered down on us. He jumped back outside the barn. Raven's whinnies got louder. I grabbed the T-post and swung it at the barn outside Raven's stall. The board splintered, but it didn't break. Tanner grabbed the post from my hands before I could swing it again and slid in under the splintered part of the board. Together, we threw our weight against the post and the board pulled away.

Raven's nose showed through the opening, but I could see flames behind him. We had to get him out of there. The air was so hot that everything looked wavy. We got a second board off, then a third, then the pony threw himself at the opening. With a splinter of wood, he charged past us as we dove out of his way.

Raven headed straight toward the fence line where Star stood quivering. With a loud crack, a piece of burning wood fell across the hole we'd opened in the side of the barn. We moved away from the heat and the flames toward the ponies.

Raven stretched his neck out and made a sound like a dog barking. Star had been out of the smoke longer, but she sounded just as bad. Cricket stood on the crest of the hill, ears pricked forward, her entire attention focused on the barn behind us. Vee, Tanner's horse, stood next to Cricket.

A cough wracked Tanner. My throat closed up and I hacked along with him. It felt like my toes had come up through my mouth by the time I caught my breath again. The ponies wouldn't let us touch them, backing away from us and making that terrible hacking sound when they took a few quick steps to get away. If my throat felt raw from the smoke outside the barn, the ponies must be worse.

"Halters," Tanner turned to go back to the barn. I grabbed his arm.

"We can't go back in there!" I could barely breathe as it was. Tanner coughed again. He looked like it hurt him as much as it did me.

I forced myself to move more slowly. When I got close enough I put my hand out to the little black mare. She stood still long enough for me to get a good look at her. Tanner had caught up with Raven, and he checked the little gelding. Star's right ear showed signs of a burn, and Raven had a red welt along the top of his flank. Both ponies were coughing constantly and had gunk coming out their noses.

We opened the gate and the ponies bolted across the field to join Cricket by the far fence. There was a water trough in that paddock. Maybe drinking would help them clear their throats. I went over and turned on the hose and took a drink myself to get rid of the awful taste of smoke. I handed the hose to Tanner so he could take a drink too. The water helped a little, but there was so much smoke in the air that I could still taste it.

Cricket had stepped on the reins and broken them, but her saddle was still in place. The reins would be expensive to replace, but I didn't care. It had been more important to get into the barn and save the ponies than to untack my horse. I pulled the tack off of her and hung it on the fence. I couldn't afford to replace those broken reins for Queenie. No way I could afford to replace a saddle.

A horse whinnied behind us.

Dressage Queen Yasmine took a picture-perfect jump over the fence. She reined Bourbon in and brought him to stand next to Cricket.

"You get through?" She swung out of the saddle.

Yasmine's phone! How was I going to tell her I'd killed it?

I opened my mouth to tell her but sirens rang out from the road. We both turned to watch. Seconds later, a fire truck roared up the lane to the barn. Another truck followed a minute later. This one had a belly filled with the water that would help them put out the fire. Firefighters poured off the truck. More vehicles skidded into the graveled area behind the tanker truck.

Volunteer firefighters suited up. They hooked the big fire hose up to the tanker truck and began to spray the barn. The heat was awful, even as far away as we were.

A pair of firefighters burst through the billowing smoke, carrying a limp form toward the firetruck parked away from the barn. A sick pit opened in my stomach. Mrs. Nelson must have been inside. I hadn't seen any sign of her when we let the ponies out.

As the firefighters rushed the woman over to the grass next to the fire engine, a sneaker fell off one of her feet. It lay bright red in the green grass.

Mom had worn her red sneakers that morning.

My breathing, harsh and difficult as it was, stopped altogether.

I was halfway down the hill when Yasmine grabbed my arm. "What are you doing?"

I shoved her aside. The outline of the fire truck flickered in and out through the thick smoke. Feet pumping, lungs filled with barb wire, I ran on.

CHAPTER ELEVEN

I dropped to my knees beside Mom. I couldn't tell how hurt she was. But she wasn't dead.

My mom was not dead.

"How did you get here?" I said.

Mom tried to answer. She winced as if the air scraped her throat. I knew exactly how she felt. A harsh cough wracked her body.

As if contagious, I coughed too.

Another siren's shrill call grew behind me, then cut off. The fire's roar was far louder than most normal sounds, so I jumped when a trio of paramedics appeared. One of the firefighters ran in the direction of the barn. The other one stayed long enough to say, "She was trapped in the feed room. It hadn't burned too much yet, but the smoke was really bad in there."

The paramedics pushed me aside so that they could work on Mom. First they rolled Mom to one side, then shoved a board underneath her and rolled her flat on top of it.

"One, two, three," the dark-haired woman said. They lifted the board and carried Mom toward the driveway. Tanner and Yasmine arrived and followed Mom with me to the waiting ambulance.

The wind blew to the south, so the air was much clearer on this side of the barn. The smoke was thin enough here that we could see the house. Mrs. Nelson and Mrs. Everett were on the front porch, holding dishtowels over their faces as they peered toward the barn. Mrs. Everett's face went white when she saw Tanner. She dropped her towel and shot down the front steps. Mrs. Nelson stooped to pick up the towel and followed Tanner's mom down to where the paramedics had shoved Mom into the ambulance.

The dark-haired woman had climbed in with her. She put a plastic mask over Mom's nose and mouth and hooked the tubing from it to a big green tank.

Mom's face looked weird behind the mask. She raised her head and started fretting with the tubing. Must be looking for me. I put a foot up on the bumper and started to climb in with her. The second paramedic stopped me, her long ponytail flipping into my face as she pulled me back down.

The force of my feet hitting the ground knocked something loose in my chest. This time the hacking brought up some really gross gunk.

Ponytail lady whipped her stethoscope off her neck and slapped it on my back. "Don't tell me you were in that barn too."

I tried to answer. When I couldn't catch enough wind to get words out, I shook my head.

"Good thing," she said. "You sound awful though. Just breathe for me, honey."

Tanner, standing a few feet away from me, started to cough so hard that he collapsed. Mrs. Everett grabbed the paramedic's arm and yanked her away from me. As she did, her purse fell off her shoulder and landed at my feet.

"Help him!" Tears ran through the ash on her face. "He said he got the ponies out; that means he was in the fire!"

The paramedic called to the dark-haired lady working on Mom, "Hand me that portable O2 tank. He's bad."

The dark-haired lady jumped down with another green tank and more green plastic tubing and another mask. The two of them fitted it onto Tanner.

"I'm calling for another bus," dark-haired lady said.

"Maybe two," Ponytail lady answered. I was wondering why they needed a bus when she pointed at me. "She doesn't look a whole lot better than he does."

I glanced down. There were small holes all over my clothes. I stuck a finger through one on my thigh.

I looked back over at Tanner. While I was coughing a lot, I could catch my breath. Tanner wasn't doing as well. While the two women worked on Tanner, I climbed into the ambulance with Mom.

Her eyes were closed, but her breathing seemed easier with the mask on. Mom's face had a bunch of crusty soot on her cheek. The hair was gone from the right side of her head, leaving nothing to hide the blisters.

Mom yelped when I reached out to brush the dirt off her face. I snatched my hand back. The black wasn't soot. It was burned skin.

Dark-haired lady crawled back inside the ambulance and told me to let her by. She pulled some gauze pads out and poured something on them. She then gently laid them over the burned areas on Mom's face and head.

"Is she going to be all right?" I asked.

"I think so. Your friend too. What were you kids doing here?" the paramedic said while she continued to work on Mom.

"The ponies were in there," I answered. "We had to get them out."

Dark-haired lady must not be a horse person because she rolled her eyes.

The spot on my shoulder where the cinder had burned through my cotton shirt hurt. I craned my neck trying to see if I had black crusts the way Mom did. I checked my face, my head, my arms. Tender yes, but smooth.

The ambulance driver came up. "You about ready to roll?" he asked.

"Gotta get both the children squared away. This one is stable enough we can wait for reinforcements to arrive. That one," she pointed at Tanner, "needs to go ASAP."

I looked past the driver as he spoke to the dark-haired lady. Mrs. Everett glanced our way. Her face was white. When she saw Mom in the ambulance her face flushed cherry red. She started to get up to come over, but Tanner grabbed her hand and tugged on it. She hesitated, then sat back down. Mrs. Nelson stood nearby, her arms wrapped around herself as she watched the fire. I could tell she was crying. Queenie and Yasmine stood with her. One of the firefighters yelled something at them, and they moved back to where the smoke wasn't so thick.

The paramedic finished his discussion and put a hand out to me. "We need to look at you. How about you come down here?"

As I climbed down from the back of the ambulance, a figure emerged from the smoke beside the barn. He ran toward the road.

My chest tightened.

Luis.

I tried to speak. Tell someone that Luis had started the fire. I couldn't draw a deep enough breath to make a sound.

I blinked, and the smoke was once again too thick to see through.

Had he really been there? Did I dream him up?

My stomach heaved. I threw up. The paramedics grabbed me and threw me inside the back of the ambulance next to Mom. Mrs. Everett's purse sailed in after me and landed on Mom's stretcher. As the engine started, ponytail lady put a mask over my face and told me to take a deep breath.

I pulled off my mask to tell her about Luis.

The paramedic put the mask back on.

Queenie called, "Don't worry about the horses. We'll take care of them."

The ambulance pulled away.

The paramedics wheeled us down a long hall once we got to the ER. Mom was in the room across from me. At least I could see her, even if it was too far away to talk to her. People wearing the ugliest green scrubs darted in and out of both rooms. They took the tubing from my face mask off the green tank marked "O2" that the paramedics had used to help me breathe. They connected the far end of the tubing to a button on the wall and twisted a dial. A fat machine rolled in. They had me sit up while they slid a "plate" behind me and took a picture of my lungs. The machine left and went into Mom's room.

A man with a funny half-shaved haircut came in and looked at my hand where I'd burned it on the door. He put some salve on it and wrapped it up.

"Press this button if you need us," the nurse said. He clipped a button that looked like a spaceship to my pillow and darted out into the hall. I was alone.

They'd left the curtains separating my little room from the hallway open. I sat up. The curtains across the way were partly shut, but I could see Mom.

She looked so still. For a second fear rose in my throat, bringing back the squeezing pain that I'd felt in the smoky barn. Then Mom's chest rose and fell. I took a breath too. She was only asleep.

Miles of electrical wires and plastic tubing led from Mom to a tower of equipment. Each of the machines had a tiny screen showing waves and patterns and numbers. I squinted to see if I could see them better. Not that I had any idea what they all meant. She must be okay or nurses would still be in there buzzing around.

Leaning back, I shifted on the hard mattress, but I couldn't get comfortable. It was cold. Distant beeps and buzzes created an unending background noise that grated on my nerves. The hospital smelled weird. An alarm sounded close by and I sat up again. One of the boxes in Mom's room beeped like a car alarm gone wild.

The nurse came in, fiddled with the tubes going from the wall to Mom. The alarm stopped. She left, tossing a smile across the way at me. What good was a smile when she ignored my frantic wave to come over and tell me how Mom was doing?

Just when I thought I'd better push my button and find out what had made the machine sound the alarm, Uncle Charlie came down the hall. His shoulders were down like he carried something heavy. When he turned his head to look at mom, a stillness came over him. Then he shook his head. Pressing his lips together, he came over to me.

"They said you're doing pretty well," he said.

"No one tells me anything." Anger bit at me. Except for the one woman who came in and turned off Mom's alarm, they hadn't come back in once since they left us alone.

"All those pretty little machines tell them that your mom is okay. They said your X-ray was pretty clear for having been in the fire. It's really dangerous to breathe in smoke."

"I wasn't in the fire. I just helped get the ponies out." Just saying that started me up again. The coughing hurt so much I thought my tonsils were coming up.

Uncle Charlie gave me a stern look. "Dr. Hales is going to come in, and if he gives the okay then you'll come home with me."

"What about Mom?" It was all well and good that my pediatrician was going to come see me, but I wanted to go home with Mom, not Uncle Charlie.

"They're keeping her for awhile." Uncle Charlie looked across at Mom. His brows drew together. She must have been awake because he went over.

No fair! I wanted to see her too. I sat up and tried to get my legs over the railing. A panel next to me started beeping.

A woman I'd never seen before ran in and yelled at me to stay in bed. She slapped a button on the bottom of the stretcher that stopped the alarm. "I'm not kidding. No getting up," she said. She didn't look like she was going to leave until I agreed. She was standing in just the wrong place and I couldn't see Mom so I nodded. She scooted out.

As I stared across at Uncle Charlie, he reached over and pulled the glass door closed.

I don't know what he actually said, but he was really mad. Mom reached up and put a hand on his arm. He got a look on his face like she'd surprised him. He leaned in and Mom half sat up, which made the beep start up again. The woman who'd turned off her alarm before went in and turned it off. This time she stayed to fiddle with a couple of things and shooed Uncle Charlie back across the hall to me. As she left, she stuck a lumpy plastic bag inside my door and told Uncle Charlie it was Mom's clothes and stuff.

Before I could grill Uncle Charlie on how Mom was and why he was so mad at her, Dr. Hales came in and pulled the curtain across the opening to the hallway.

"Well now, how's my favorite patient?"

He said this to everyone. It still made me flush a little. I loved my pediatrician.

Dr. Hales pulled a bunch of stuff out of a cabinet and made me blow in a tube then suck in big breaths while he put his stethoscope on my back. Then I had to listen to both him and Uncle Charlie tell me never ever to go near a burning building ever, ever again. I'd already promised Uncle Charlie, but I promised Dr. Hales, too. Considering how much it hurt to breathe, it was easy to agree.

When he was done, Dr. Hales opened the curtain and motioned for Uncle Charlie to follow him. The space across the way where Mom had been was empty.

I fumbled the call button down and pressed it over and over.

"What can we do for you?" came the voice from the wall again.

"Where did you take my mom?" My voice wasn't very quiet, and Uncle Charlie came back in.

"It's okay," he told the wall. "I'm back in with Sophie. I'll explain."

Turned out Mom had been taken to a place called the burn unit. Despite what I thought were pretty convincing arguments about how we needed to go see Mom right then, I still found myself in a wheelchair, carrying Mom's bag of clothes while being pushed out to the exit where Uncle Charlie waited in Mom's car that he'd picked up from the Nelsons's.

CHAPTER TWELVE

Uncle Charlie wasn't listening. We needed to go back to the hospital to be with Mom. Instead he'd driven me home. He steered the car into my driveway.

"Why are we here?" I interrupted my own tirade to ask.

"Your mom needs some things. I'll drop you off at Yasmine's when I run them back to the hospital."

I huffed out of the car and slammed my door.

"You're going to have to be careful for the next few days," Uncle Charlie said when even that tiny amount of effort earned me a coughing fit that left me leaning on the side of the car for support.

I glared at him. "If Mom needs "things," then why did the nurses give us all of her clothes?" I asked.

"Cut it out," Uncle Charlie's voice was low and tired.

Let him get stuff for Mom, I'd go with him when he took it to her. I walked around to the trunk of the car and pulled on it. "I need my backpack," I said.

"What?" He sounded startled.

"My backpack's in the trunk." I gave him a funny look. He sure was acting weird.

I waggled my bandaged hand in the air. "Can you bring it inside for me?"

"Go see to the dog," he said. "I'll bring your pack."

He was right. I needed to calm Misty down. She barked hysterically behind the back gate because we weren't petting her yet. As soon I opened it, she leapt up and sloppy-licked my face. Her claws caught in the plastic bags holding Mom's and my stuff and I fought her off. Then Misty spotted Uncle Charlie, shoved past me, and raced to give him the welcome treatment. The dog hit him and Uncle Charlie nearly dropped the gas can he had lifted out of the trunk.

"What's that?" The words blurted out. I already knew the answer. It was the can of gas for the mower we kept next to the trash cans. It had no business anywhere near the trunk of the car.

"Inside," Uncle Charlie growled at me.

Misty backed away. I grabbed the dog's collar and shoved her back inside the gate and shut it.

"Why was our gas can in the trunk?" My voice rose.

Uncle Charlie was at my side in an instant. He gripped the top of my shoulder, causing pain to ricochet down my arm. "Keep your voice down. Now go in the house while I put this away." Uncle Charlie's face was twisted with an emotion I'd never seen there before. He was afraid.

Like Mom had been.

An unfamiliar dark feeling threatened to choke me like the smoke from the burning barn. Shaken, I fled.

Once in the kitchen, I tossed the bag of Mom's things from the hospital by the door and grabbed a glass out of the cabinet. I stuck it under the spout on the fridge. The ice clattered more loudly than usual. Or maybe it was because my hand was shaking so much that the cubes bounced around in the glass. I put my other hand around the glass and willed them to hold still. The ice settled.

Uncle Charlie came in and closed the door behind him.

"Sit," he said.

I took the glass to the table, pulled out my chair, and sat. Misty barked once, then sat when Uncle Charlie patted her on the head. He handed me my backpack, then walked over and sat in Mom's chair.

"Look, I'm sorry I yelled at you. I needed to put that can back where it belongs before someone saw it and misunderstood."

"It wasn't in the trunk when we got to the barn," I said.

"I figured as much," Uncle Charlie said, eyes on the door behind me. "Don't read too much into it," he said. "But don't mention it to anyone either."

Our eyes locked. I got what he wasn't saying. *"Don't tell or else your mom is in deep trouble."*

I nodded. "Is that what caused the fire in the barn?"

"I have no idea," Uncle Charlie said. "Fortunately, I went to the car to get some stuff out before the fire marshal thought to look inside it."

"The other night, I thought raccoons were messing with the trash. Could it have been somebody stealing that gas can?" I asked. "We usually keep them both in the corner."

Uncle Charlie's eyebrows shot up. He bent forward and kissed me on the forehead. "Could very well be. Why don't you get washed up, pack a few things, and we'll go see if we can sneak you in to see your mother before I run you over to Yasmine's. Then we're going to call your dad."

"No!" jerked out of me.

"No to spending the night with Yasmine, or no to calling your Dad?"

"We don't need to call Dad, do we?"

When Uncle Charlie looked surprised, which he would because I really like my dad, I added. "Not yet anyway. Let's wait 'til we see Mom."

Uncle Charlie nodded.

I started to go up to have a shower, but then remembered what the nurse had said as he wheeled me out of the ER. "Don't get this wet. Your doctor will change it when he sees you in a couple of days."

Uncle Charlie helped me tape a plastic grocery sack over my burned hand so I could take a shower without getting the dressing wet. I went upstairs.

The steam in the hot shower made me cough harder and deeper at first, but I actually felt pretty good after I hacked up another bunch of gunk that Uncle Charlie didn't need to know about. Back in my room, I took a better look at my clothes. Mom really would kill me when she got home. If she came home.

The darkness rose inside me again. I stuck a finger in one of the holes in the thigh of the pants and ripped them apart. The pants fell to the floor as I shook my hands, as if I could fling off all the crazy feelings I had piled up inside me.

I threw myself on the bed. Face pressed against the quilt, my breath shuddered in and out. Queenie's advice sounded in my head. *Breathe, child. Slow and steady. In, two, three, four. Out, two, three, four.* I took one deep breath, then another. The dark feeling was still there, but my brain came back online. I got up and pulled a clean T-shirt out of the drawer and grabbed jeans off the hanger in my closet. Tee and pants? Check. I needed shoes. My feet slipped into my flip flops. Grabbing Yasmine's cell phone, I headed out the door.

Uncle Charlie was moving around in Mom's room, packing what looked like an awful lot of clothes. I didn't want to know how long he thought Mom would stay in the hospital so I went on downstairs.

Misty was lying on the rag rug in the kitchen. I flopped down and scratched her belly. The bag with Mom's stuff in it had fallen off Mom's chair. Mrs. Everett's purse had fallen out of the bag, contents sliding out of the open top onto the floor. I should have told the nurses to give it back to Mrs. Everett in the E.R. She must have been there with Tanner, although I hadn't seen them. I picked up the wallet and other things to stuff them back in. Inside were a couple of computer printouts. A note in the margin of the top one caught my eye.

The pencil had all but torn the paper. *Did you order these things? Why did we pay for them if we never got them in?* Mr. Nelson wrote that. He'd left Yasmine and me enough babysitting notes that I recognized the big block lettering.

Shuffling through the pages, I found more notations, some in Mom's writing, some in Mr. Nelson's. There were other pages with darker print. The notes on these pages were different. They said similar things, but all questioned

Jaimie's—my mother's—decisions in ordering the items. I didn't recognize the writing. The pages rustled like old leaves as my hands dropped to my lap. Misty stuck her wet nose under my hand, and I lifted it automatically to stroke the top of her head while I thought. Luis was at the Nelsons' and could have put the gas can in Mom's car. I stopped petting Misty and checked the dates on the notations. They happened after Luis had left the store. *Did that mean Luis wasn't the one who stole from the store?*

This had to be the evidence Mrs. Everett said she had that proved Mom had stolen from the store. The front doorbell rang. Papers still in hand, I walked toward the front door. When I got to the front room, I saw the flash of a uniform outside.

When I turned around, all I could see was the tuft of accounting pages sticking up out of Mom's work bag. I didn't hesitate, but snatched then up and added them to the pile of papers from Mrs. Everett's purse. Then I ran up the stairs. Dad could let the police in.

Door closed firmly behind me, I ran over and tugged open the door to my closet. Holding the monster-warning bell in one hand, I quietly opened the door to my secret room. Scrambling across the floor, I lifted the flap on Chester's side and thrust the pages inside.

There was a knock on my bedroom door. I scooted back out into the closet, and then closed the secret room door. As I tugged the clothes back across the rack, Uncle Charlie opened the door and stuck his head in.

"The fire marshal's here." His face was grim. "They have a warrant to search the house."

"But they'll find—"

"There's nothing to find, Bug. Nothing that hasn't been here all along."

I carefully didn't look like I'd hidden evidence either.

"I'll be down in just a minute."

Uncle Charlie nodded and left. His footsteps clattered down the stairs as I made sure the clothes covered the opening to the secret room. When they looked okay, I followed him.

A blonde lady in a firefighter's uniform stood in the kitchen, a folded piece of paper in her hands. Two men stood behind her.

I caught Misty's collar as she tried to jump on the woman.

"Good dog." She held out her hand to me. "Fire Marshal Deborah Saums."

I didn't want to shake her hand. I looked up at Uncle Charlie. My fear had to show in my face because both Uncle Charlie and the fire marshal's faces changed. Worse, my throat closed up again and I began to hack.

"I need to get the little one to the hospital," Uncle Charlie said. "The car's out back, we'll get out of your way if that's all right."

I looked up at Uncle Charlie. I'd already been treated, but he'd made it sound like I was in dire need of medical attention. I stuck the hand with the bandage on it behind my back.

"Of course. Stubbs?" the fire marshal called one of her men over. "Go check the car. Make it quick, though, so they can get to the ER."

After a small hesitation, Uncle Charlie handed over the keys to the Rabbit.

She searched both the bag he'd packed for Mom, and my backpack, then waved us on through the kitchen to the back door. For a moment, all the adults turned their back on me. I snatched up Mrs. Everett's purse and stuffed it into my backpack.

One of the investigators went up the stairs. What if he found my secret room? The papers I'd taken from Mrs. Everett could get Mom into a ton of trouble.

Stress tightened my throat. I started to cough.

"I really need to get her to the hospital," Uncle Charlie said.

"I'm okay." Talking made me cough harder. If they found the gas or the papers, we were all in trouble.

I was surprised when the man returned and the fire marshal told him to hand Uncle Charlie the keys to the car. I'd been so sure they'd find a way to arrest him over that stupid can of gas.

We got in the Rabbit and pulled out of the driveway. All I could do was hope our luck held and they didn't go in the crawl space.

CHAPTER THIRTEEN

"We should have stayed." My jaw ached. During the divorce, my dentist had told Mom and Dad I needed something else that would bring my anger and stress down to a dull roar. I'd taken up chewing on my nails. This turned out to drive everyone else crazy, but didn't hurt my teeth. Today I'd been doing a lot of both.

Uncle Charlie rammed the gas pedal and took the turn into the parking lot a little too fast. "When we were at the hospital, you didn't want to leave. Now you're not even interested in seeing your mom."

At my quick intake of breath, he barreled on over my objection, "As I've told you twenty-eleven times. Somebody put that gasoline in your mom's car to point the investigation in her direction. Putting it back where it belongs? Makes it like it never happened."

He carefully pulled the car into a parking space and switched off the engine.

"Luis did it." I blurted. Putting both hands on my knees, I twisted in my seat to face my uncle.

"What?" Uncle Charlie sounded startled. "Queenie's Luis? Why would he do that?"

"The Nelsons fired him at the store. Maybe he held a grudge."

Uncle Charlie drummed his fingers on the steering wheel before he spoke. "Your mom is the one who recommended him to Queenie. She wouldn't have done that if she thought he was stealing from the store. He has no reason to set those fires, much less make it seem like your mom did it."

"But I found rags that smelled like gasoline in his trunk."

"You went snooping in the car of some guy you think burned down a building?" One of Uncle Charlie's hands tightened on the steering wheel as he whipped his face toward me. "What are you thinking?"

"Nobody was doing anything."

This time it was Uncle Charlie's jaw that clenched. "Just because we don't consult you doesn't mean we aren't actually doing something."

I took in a gulp of air. I'd been worried sick, and they hadn't told me anything. And now I was the one in trouble. "What if they find out the gas from our can started that fire? You *and* Mom will go to jail and I'll get sent to California." I slipped one arm into my backpack straps as I got out and slammed the door.

Uncle Charlie climbed out and looked at me across the top of the car. "So that's why you didn't want to call your dad. Look, your mom didn't do this, and she's not going to jail." He turned to walk toward the hospital. Clearly he thought we were done talking. I wanted to argue, but it took all the breath I had to keep up with his big stride. That was the most unfair way to end an argument an adult had ever used on me.

Once inside, we stopped at the information desk. A big woman with even bigger iron-gray curls sat behind the desk. She checked her computer for Mom's room, and gave us directions to the burn unit. The lady licked her pencil, then wrote a room number down on a slip of paper that she handed to me. I took it between two fingertips, grossed out by that whole pencil licking thing. Uncle Charlie thanked her and took the note from me. He asked another question and I walked over to the seats. Plopping down under the weight of my backpack, I had an idea. Easing Mrs. Everett's purse out I slid it under the chair.

Uncle Charlie turned and waved for me to come with him. I wasn't sure leaving that purse there was the right thing to do. All I could do was hope that someone honest found it and turned it in. This way she would never know that I had found it first. The evidence she'd had was hidden now, as long as the fire marshall didn't find it.

The minute the elevator doors opened on Mom's floor, I forgot everything but how wrong it smelled, rotten under the fresh pine scent. I reached for Uncle Charlie's hand. He held tight. The hallway seemed to get longer as we walked down it, but we finally arrived at Mom's room.

The door was open. Uncle Charlie let go of my hand to give Mom a hug.

I hung back. All those wires and tubes surrounded Mom like a thicket. Pretty sure if I got any closer, I might break something.

"Sophie?" Mom looked like she was going to cry. She held her hand out and I went over and made myself reach for her hand. I could feel the bones lying under her skin, like she'd dried up in the fire.

My throat closed up. I just knew if I tried to talk I'd start coughing again.

"I'm glad you got here in time." Mom's voice was husky. "They're going to put a tube in my throat, just in case, to help me breathe."

I nodded like that was fine. But it wasn't. I looked up at Uncle Charlie, silently begging him to make this better.

Uncle Charlie put his hand on my shoulder. "Sophie, your mom and I need to talk," he said. He was still pretending I didn't know what was going on.

Mom pulled me down for a quick hard hug. I kissed her cheek quickly and pulled back, making sure I didn't take any tubes or wires with me.

Mom's eyes cut to Uncle Charlie's face, then back to mine.

"I won't be long," Uncle Charlie said. "Wait down by the nurses' station."

They might not want to worry me, but I needed to know what was going on. I'd be right outside, with the door open a crack.

Big surprise. They were talking about the gas can.

"I told you. As far as I know it's been in our garage all along," Mom said.

Who took that gas can? Luis? Mrs. Everett? Mr. Nelson? I caught myself raising my finger to my mouth and whipped it down to my side. If I broke this bad habit, maybe it would help Mom get better.

"Sophie saw it when I took it out of the car."

"No wonder she didn't want to be here, she thinks I did this." Raw pain laced Mom's words.

"What? No!" Uncle Charlie said. "I told her someone put that can in your car. She thinks it was Luis."

I couldn't hear Mom's response to that because one of the nurses came by. She pushed a plastic cart with one of the squeakiest wheels ever made. When the nurse got far enough down the hall for me to hear again, Mom had changed topics.

"I wouldn't even have been there if Katy Nelson hadn't asked me to feed the ponies for her. She had to run the twins to their piano lesson," she said.

Uncle Charlie sighed. "You know how that looks."

"How as I supposed to know that someone would burn down the building." Mom's voice sounded like Uncle Charlie's truck driving over the gravel on our driveway. "I thought I was doing a favor for a friend."

"Would Katy have sent you over there knowing that the barn would go up in flames?"

"Katy? Are you crazy?" Mom said. The nurse and the squeaky wheeled cart passed going the other way and I missed what she said next.

Uncle Charlie spoke up, "So the question now becomes who else knew you were going to the Nelsons'."

"And who would set a fire when I was in—" Mom's coughing was pretty bad this time.

Uncle Charlie said something about getting a nurse. I took a step away.

"Water," Mom croaked out.

Ice cubes clattered in a cup, then a long silence.

"What did Daniel say when you called him?"

"I haven't. You know how it's been," Mom said. "If I call him, he might..."

Mom was afraid Dad would take me. I was right to worry.

My parents hadn't been very nice to one another during the divorce. At first they were really adult about it, sat me down, told me it was not my fault, it was them. All those "right" things the magazines told them to do.

But then Mom would say "your father" like it was a dirty word. Dad would take me out to dinner and show me pictures of a barn in California that he'd picked out for me. It was my worst day even when they sat me down and told me I got to choose which one I'd live with. I didn't want to choose between them. After a week of no sleep and worrying about everything, I'd told them I wanted to stay where I'd always lived. Dad had flung himself out of the house, and while he was nice to me when I came to visit him and he didn't pressure me to come live with him, he wasn't always that nice to Mom.

A beep sounded in Mom's room. Uncle Charlie's voice got louder as he said Mom's name over and over. A nurse ran down the hall and through Mom's door.

Uncle Charlie came out. He looked spooked.

Another nurse came down the hall fast. The cart she pushed nearly fell over when she turned and went inside Mom's room.

Uncle Charlie grabbed my arm and marched toward the elevator.

"What's going on?" I struggled to free myself from his grip.

"She's having some trouble. They're going to have to put that tube in. Then she'll be safe."

I didn't want Mom safe. I wanted her well, and home.

The fire marshal lady stepped out of the elevator. A man in uniform followed her down the hall. Both Uncle Charlie and I stopped dead. In her hand were a bunch of papers. My heart sank. They must have found the accounting sheets with Mr. Nelson's questions on them. And the lighter. I closed my eyes and wished with all my might that I'd never looked in Luis's car. I'd made it worse. Now the lighter that might have started the fire was in our house.

The woman came up to us. "Is Ms. Allen feeling better?"

Uncle Charlie had his eyes on the papers in her hand, same as me. They looked funny, with stamps and stuff on them. Words caught my eye. "Arrest Warrant." Not the accounting sheets. But something far worse.

His answer came out in a harsh voice. "They're putting a breathing tube in right now. She's going to be here a while. You'll have time to find out who really did this before you arrest her."

"I'm sorry," The fire marshal began.

"Mom's not guilty," I said.

The fire marshal looked down at me. Her face had the same look of pity that Yasmine's had held at the fire. I wanted to scratch it off.

"Go find out what's going on with Ms. Allen," the fire marshal told the man with her.

I started to block his way, but Uncle Charlie herded me away.

"Stay here." He nodded his head at a chair in the waiting room. Pulling out his phone, he punched a bunch of buttons. After a minute of squinting at the screen and scrolling, he mashed on the screen, then brought the phone to his ear.

"Hello. I need to hire a criminal attorney."

Uncle Charlie dropped me off at Yasmine's house, then went back up to the hospital. I'd been able to go in to see Mom before we left, but I kind of wish I hadn't. The thicket of wires and tubes had grown until her entire face was covered. Mom hadn't woken up, even when I leaned over the bed and hugged her. Uncle Charlie had explained that the new machine would breathe for Mom and help to clean her lungs while she got better and that they'd given her medicine to help her sleep while the breathing machine was on. I was glad they had. I'd have nightmares if they did that to me.

Yasmine and her dad met us at the door. My friend's face crumpled when I handed her phone back to her and told her what had happened. Mr. Sungupta gulped, but said he would take care of getting her a new phone the next day.

Uncle Charlie left and we joined Mrs. Sengupta in the kitchen, where she stirred a wonderful smelling curry on the stove. She started being motherly, which made me feel like crying. Not going to happen in that crowd. I turned and ran upstairs to Yasmine's room.

She followed me.

After I got myself back in control, I caught Yasmine up on the events since leaving the barn.

After a couple of clearing-of-her-throat sounds, my friend finally spoke. "They searched your house? And they arrested your mom? Have you thought about the possibility—"

"Excuse me?" I interrupted.

Yasmine looked away. When she replied her tone came out a little too forced. "Of course she didn't do it. It's just," She stopped, blew out a breath that sounded almost like a raspberry. "You're a smart girl, Sophie. It looks bad. Not that I'm saying she did it," Yasmine added hastily.

I started to get angry, but then the vision of that gas can and those papers swam into my mind. I shoved it away. Yasmine wasn't the only one thinking the wrong thing.

"Have you heard anything about Tanner?" I changed the subject.

"They let him go home," Yasmine said.

"You called him?"

"Tanner called me." A blush spread over Yasmine's face.

"He's okay?" I hoped I got some of my friend-karma back by not mentioning her blush.

"The doctor told him he can go back to school on Monday. But no riding. We might have to cancel our lesson tomorrow with both you and Tanner out." Yasmine looked crushed.

"Dr. Hales didn't say not to ride. Besides, I need to talk to Queenie," I said.

"Luis didn't set that fire either," Yasmine crossed her arms across her chest. "Queenie said he came over with her."

I smoothed the blanket under the foot of the mattress. "I don't care what Queenie said. Luis did it."

Yasmine shook her head before she turned away. "We should go down for supper," she said.

We trooped down the steps. As soon as I saw the carefully blank expressions on the Sengupta's faces as they sat around their tidy dinner table, I knew they all thought my mother was guilty.

My throat closed up. Struggling for breath. I whirled and pounded back up the steps. Yasmine's door slammed behind me. Pulling my phone out, I punched up Uncle's Charlie's number.

The call connected. "I want to call you back, so leave me a message." How could my uncle's recorded voice sound so normal when the world was coming apart?

"Uncle Charlie—" I broke off and ended the call. He'd left me to go help Mom. I couldn't get in the way of that.

CHAPTER FOURTEEN

Yasmine slipped into her room as I put my phone back in my hip pocket. Uncle Charlie would call back eventually. Or not. My message hadn't sounded as desperate as I felt.

"Parents look like guilty puppies when they're worried." Yasmine's eyes puckered in disgust as she sat down beside me.

The image of fierce, dark Mr. Sengupta looking like a bad dog broke something free inside me and I hiccuped with laughter.

The memory of Mom so still in the middle of all those machines stopped my giggles.

"They're really going to arrest her. How can that even happen?" I hugged my knees to my chest. Yasmine scooted over so that her shoulder pressed against mine. The warmth helped as much as her joke had. My world was crashing, but I wasn't alone.

"Uncle Charlie's probably still with your Mom. She's in the hospital, not jail, so you know she's being taken care of," Yasmine continued our hour-long argument.

We'd hunkered down in her room. Curry-smeared plates sat on the floor next to the trundle, the taste still on my tongue. Mrs. Sengupta had brought them up when it was clear that we weren't coming back down for supper. I hadn't thought I could eat, but had felt better for filling my stomach with the savory chicken, potatoes, raisins, and peppers.

"Uncle Charlie doesn't know the lawyers Dad knows. If I call him, he can get Mom a better lawyer."

Yasmine looked away. She didn't have to repeat what she'd said ten times before. If I called Dad, he'd come, and California might be on the table again.

I bit my pinkie finger, the only one that still had any nail left to chew on.

Yasmine batted it out of my mouth. "If you call him, and he makes you move, then I'm stuck here, alone. No one was my friend before you started talking to me."

"You won't be stuck. You'll have Kilby, and lots of people like you."

"They tolerate me. Don't you remember how people treated me before we got to be friends?"

I looked sideways at her. To me she was just Yasmine, the funniest, fiercest friend I would ever have. Then the curry smell tickled my nose. The dishes that at first seemed exotic were strangely comforting now. Her family *had* seemed foreign until I got to know them. She was right. People still looked at her funny sometimes, but surely now that people knew her it would be okay.

My phone rang.

"I was with your Mom when you called and couldn't pick up right then." Uncle Charlie sounded wrung out.

"How is Mom?"

He hesitated. "Asleep. She's more comfortable that way. I'm still working on getting her a decent lawyer."

"Working on getting her a lawyer?" My voice squeaked into a higher octave. "You haven't found one yet?"

"She made me promise not to call your father." Uncle Charlie's voice had a rough edge. "We may need his connections."

My gaze flew up to meet Yasmine's. Her eyes widened. She'd heard.

"What..." Truth was, there were so many questions whirling around in my brain that I would never be able to ask the right one first. The papers I'd hidden in Chester's belly were weighing heavy on me. Were they still at home, or were they at the fire station?

"Can you come get me?"

"Look, Bug, I'll pick you up in the morning and take you home so you can grab what you need for another day at Yasmine's. You'll need to plan to go to school with her on Monday. Meanwhile, you tell the Senguptas thanks from your mom. She really appreciated knowing that you were set."

"But—"

"It's been a long day. Get some rest and I'll call you in the morning after I see your mom."

"But—," I began again.

"Love you, kiddo."

The call ended. My hand dropped to my lap and I fiddled with the phone, turning it on, then off, then on again. Uncle Charlie hadn't told me anything really. Asleep. What did that mean? Was Mom better? Worse?

Yasmine's hand dropped over my fidgeting fingers. "You can't do anything for her right now," she said.

I decided. "I can call Dad."

Yasmine's mouth turned down.

"I don't want to move, but I have to do something."

She dropped her gaze.

I took that to mean okay. Punching up Dad's number, I pressed the button to call.

"Sophie!" Dad answered on the second ring.

My eyes stung because he sounded so happy.

"Daddy, I need you to help me with something important."

"Sure thing. Homework?"

"Mom..." My throat closed up. I cleared it. "We need a good lawyer."

"Was there an accident? Are you okay?" The tone he used was the same one I'd heard when I was little and skinned my knee.

"I'm fine, Dad. It's Mom. I think she's going to have to go to jail."

"What happened?" His voiced morphed from Dad to lawyer just that fast.

I told him.

He agreed to make some calls and said he'd be on the red-eye flight that would get him back to Maryland by the next morning.

My hand shook a little when I pressed "end." Yasmine had backed up so that she was on the opposite end of the trundle from me. It had gone about as well as I could have hoped for. Dad was going to help Mom.

And he hadn't said a thing about California.

Yet.

Yasmine and I sat a few feet apart from one another on the front porch the next morning. She hadn't spoken to me since I made the call the night before. She wouldn't listen when I tried to explain. Up 'til then I'd assumed that even if I had to move, even if I wasn't in Maryland, we could still be friends. I'd thought nothing could hurt worse than seeing my mother lying on the grass by the burning barn. I was wrong. Having my best friend stop talking to me was just as bad.

Dad drove up. I launched myself off the step. He and I took the last few steps toward each other at a run like some corny commercial. He swept me up into a huge hug. The scratch of the not-yet-shaved face and the smell of the suit where I'd buried my face made my eyes tear up. I sure had missed him.

He moved his hands to my shoulders and met my gaze with a steady look. "You did the right thing calling me. I can help," he looked past me and straightened. "This must be Yasmine."

Dad reached out a hand to shake. Yasmine glared up at him. She made him wait for it, but she finally took his hand and shook.

The Senguptas came out on the stoop to met Dad. I'd already said, "Thank you," but as soon as Dad opened his mouth and said, "Thanks for watching her," big surprise, Mrs. Sengupta wanted to talk. I have never been able to get away from her quickly, but Dad was great. We backed out of their driveway ten minutes after he drove up.

I looked back.

Yasmine had already gone back inside.

I turned to face the street.

Dad hit the turn signal and steered the car toward our house. "I got off the phone with Charlie a few minutes ago. He said your mother was stable. The plan is to take you home, then I'll meet a friend who does criminal work at the hospital. She wants to talk to your mother and get some idea what is going on."

"So Mom's okay? That tube they put in worked and her lungs are better?"

Dad took the corner slow and didn't answer.

"Dad?" I reached over and grabbed his arm.

"She's going to have the tube in for a couple more days," Dad said. "But she is better today than she was last night."

"How can she talk to the lawyer with the tube in?"

"We'll work something out." Dad shook the arm I still clutched. The glance he gave me told me he needed it to drive.

I let go.

We talked about stuff that didn't matter much the rest of the way home. The good news was that he would stay with me until Mom got out of the hospital, so I could be at home. Dad dropped me off and went to talk to Mom.

It was weird when I got into my room and found stuff still neat but moved around. My skin itched when I looked at the dresser drawers they hadn't bothered to close. I hauled my laundry basket over and dumped everything from my drawers into the basket. I was not wearing clothes they'd pawed through.

The closet door was open. Stuff was moved, but nothing tossed around. I shoved my clothes over and pulled open the crawl space door. I walked over to Chester and slid my hand inside his belly. Fingers ruffled through the loose sheets of paper. My breath whooshed out. They hadn't found the secret space. I pulled the papers out.

Back in my room, I smoothed out the quilt and spread the sheets of paper on my bed.

An hour later, I still didn't know what they meant. I snapped a couple of photos and sent them to Kilby. Her mom was a bookkeeper, and Mom trusted her. Maybe she would understood this stuff.

I waited. And waited. After five minutes, when I still hadn't heard anything back from my friend, I tried to call. No answer.

I called Yasmine, only realizing how dumb that was when I got her voice mail. Her dad was going to take her to get a new phone, but the store had only just opened and they probably hadn't set her phone up yet. I went ahead and left a message. "Hey, I found something weird. Call me, okay?"

I slid my phone back in my hip pocket and glared at the accounting lines. Mrs. Everett's pages were way different from Mom's. How was I supposed to now which ones were the "cooked" ones? None of it made any sense to me, and the comments in Mr. Nelson's handwriting still scared me.

Laundry basket hefted under one arm, I made my way down to the washer. Once I had a load in, I tried Yasmine again. She still didn't pick up.

"Call me!" I said to her voice mail. She should have the new phone working by now. Surely she wasn't still mad.

I hung up and dialed Dad.

He answered. "Lawyer's here. You get some lunch?" He sounded tense.

"Mom's okay?" I looked at the papers spread out on the floor in front of me. She needed to get better. I had some questions for her to answer.

"She's okay. Uncomfortable." He must have covered the mic on the phone because his next words were muffled.

"What?" I said.

More words I couldn't quite make out, then his voice cleared up. "I have to go. I'll call you when I'm on my way back home."

A year ago I would have given anything to hear that from Dad. Now all I could think was that maybe home for me would be that modern house out in California.

I lifted the phone again and punched in Yasmine's number. *Please answer.*

One ring. Then two, three, four rings. It clicked over to voice mail.

I didn't bother with a message.

CHAPTER FIFTEEN

Yasmine had been right. Calling Dad was a mistake. But not for the reason she'd said. I'd forgotten how hard he was to convince when he was wrong about something.

"I'm not a kid anymore." Fists on my hips, I glared at Dad. Our deal the night before was that since it was too late to go back to see Mom, he'd take me there in the morning. But now, after I'd found him breakfast to hurry things along, he told me that children didn't belong in hospitals.

Uncle Charlie was way easier to get around.

Good thing he'd driven up while Dad and I were discussing things.

My uncle stood at the foot of the back steps, cleared his throat, and exchanged a glance with Dad. My eyes narrowed when Uncle Charlie's shoulders went up, then down, in a clear "I'm not getting between you two" shrug.

"How 'bout I take you to the barn this morning after you see Dr. Hales and get that dressing changed," my uncle finally offered.

Dad nodded like he thought this was a great idea.

"No."

Both of them stared. Good. I'd never turned down going to the barn before, but this was the time to do it. They needed to pay attention to me.

"I want to see Mom."

Dad squatted down. Grownups think it makes them friendlier to kids when their face is down on our level. Thing is, Dad didn't realize how much I'd grown that year. His face was about two feet lower than mine.

"I'm going," I said.

"No. You're not." He played his last card: the me-grown-up, you-kid one. He stood up, nodded at Uncle Charlie, and picked up the keys to Mom's car.

Uncle Charlie's strong fingers closed around my arm when I started to follow Dad. He let go only after the sound of the car faded.

"Dr. Hales, then the barn," my uncle said.

I stalked past Uncle Charlie and got in his truck.

We pulled in the lane at Queenie's. It was the last place I wanted to be. Yasmine wasn't speaking to me. It wasn't my day with Cricket, and Mom, in the hospital, could be dying for all I knew.

Uncle Charlie's advice for how to deal with the boarders who believed Mrs. Everett's accusations? Hold your head up.

Not incredibly helpful.

I went to find Queenie to see if she had some tack I could clean. If I had to be there, I might as well see if I could earn some money.

"Let's see," my trainer said when I found her. "There's a barrel of old tack I've been meaning to put up for sale on the website. If you clean it, take photos, and upload them to my computer, I can call that done."

"Thanks!" I went to work.

Two hours later, my back hurt, my fingers looked like prunes, the bandage Dr. Hales had put on looked filthy and would need to be redone, but I'd cleaned and photographed six bridles. I'd seen Yasmine pass by the office, but she didn't come in. I didn't go after her either. If she didn't want to be friends anymore there wasn't anything I could say or do about it.

I finished sending Queenie the photographs of the bridles when I saw her coming toward the office. Mrs. Everett stopped the trainer outside the door.

I slipped off the chair so that I was hidden by the table where I'd been cleaning the tack. After a second, I stuck my head around the side of the desk so I could keep an eye on things.

Queenie saw me and tugged at the bill of her baseball cap, but it didn't hide the twitch of her lips as she hid a grin.

Mrs. Everett asked, "Did you happen to see my purse at my brothers after the fire? It's missing."

I felt kind of bad. If someone found that purse, they sure hadn't turned it in. I hadn't meant for her to lose the whole thing.

"No, I'm sorry. I haven't," Queenie said. "Did you try the fire department?"

"They didn't have it."

"Good luck," Queenie said. "Replacing purses, and all the things we keep inside, is tough."

"In this case, it's critical." Mrs. Everett walked away.

Queenie came into the office. "Clear to come out."

I stood up and dusted off the knees of my jeans.

She directed her attention to the bridles I'd cleaned. "Those look good enough to keep. Good job."

"Does that mean I've earned a bonus?" I asked.

Queenie's eyes crinkled as she smiled. Then her face got thoughtful. She reached behind her and closed the door.

"Sit." She pointed at the chair in front of her desk. "Yasmine said that you had some questions about Luis."

"He was there, at the Nelsons' barn. I saw him. And he had stuff that could start a fire in his car." I shifted my weight but stayed standing. Yasmine didn't approve of my investigating. What was she doing talking to Queenie about Luis?

"I want you to think about what you're saying." Queenie's face was still.

I stared at her. "I saw him. He was there!" My voice echoed off the hard concrete block walls of her office.

Queenie's lips pressed together. She focused on my face and spoke. "That boy was *here*, working hard as usual, all day when the fire at Nelson's Tack broke out. He never left the property. I know this because I had to give him a ride to work and a ride home that day because his car broke down. He was mucking your horse's stall when I got the call about the fire at the Nelsons' barn. He rode over there with me because I thought we might need help with those ponies. Luis was the one who brought Cricket and the ponies safely back here and took care of them after you and your mom and Tanner got taken care of."

I swallowed hard and looked down at my toes. Queenie never lied, but Luis had to be guilty. If he wasn't, then those papers Mrs. Everett had in her bag might be real and Mom... My head came up. I was not going there.

"They had to fire him—" I began.

Queenie cut me off. Her next words were clipped. "Mrs. Everett thought he'd done something wrong. If you think hard enough, you can see where she might accuse the wrong person and then not be able to recognize when she's wrong."

"But..." Again I couldn't finish what I wanted to say.

"Your mom didn't set those fires and neither did Luis," Queenie said. "Leave the investigating to the fire department. They'll find the right person without your help."

I dropped my gaze to the floor and thought hard.

My phone buzzed in my pocket. Still not looking Queenie in the eyes, I pulled it out. Uncle Charlie.

Queenie nodded at me to answer.

"Hello?" I said.

"Ready to go home?" he asked. "Your dad called and said he'd meet us at your house in a half-hour."

"I'll meet you at the truck," I closed the call and pushed my phone back in my pocket.

"Go on," Queenie said. "But I want you to think about what I've said. Don't go making the same mistake Nancy Everett has done with your mom. Accusing that young man of arson could ruin him."

I got it. This time I didn't meet Queenie's eyes because I was ashamed.

"Think about it." Queenie stood up. "Good job on the tack."

"Thanks."

I left with six times five dollars paid toward Cricket's lease, and a whole lot of hard thinking to do.

Uncle Charlie dropped me off at home after he'd read me the riot act about getting my bandage so dirty, then left to meet a client. I do my best thinking on horseback, but my second favorite place to think was in the shower. I stripped off the bandage that had offended Uncle Charlie so much, started the hot water and climbed in. I'd clean everything and then rewrap it myself.

The water felt good, but it couldn't distract me from the problems I had. If Luis didn't do it, who did? My eyes cut toward where my phone sat on the sink out of the way of any splashing water. Talking to Yasmine would sure be helpful. Too bad she wasn't speaking to me.

The key had to be in those pages that had been in Mrs. Everett's purse. I scrubbed the tack junk out from under my nails and cut the shower short. I needed to take a closer look and figure that out before Dad got home. I grabbed some wound cream and gauze wrap from the bathroom medicine cabinet and took care of my hand. Good thing we'd had an unmounted session on wound care a few weeks before at our Pony Club meeting so I knew what to do.

I wasn't sure when Dad would show up so I locked my bedroom door. I got the pages out of the secret room and spread them on my bed.

My eyes lit on the page with Mr. Nelson's handwriting on it. I picked it up. "Explain this!" his note said.

Someone rattled the doorknob. I snatched up the pages and stuffed them under my bed.

I went over and unlocked the door. Dad stood there. His smile was forced. Something was wrong.

"What happened to Mom?" I said.

"They said she's making great progress. Should be able to come off that ventilator tomorrow."

I sank onto my bed and folded my arms across my chest. That wasn't good enough.

Dad shifted his weight. "That's really fast for as badly burned as she was."

I got up and hugged him. "I'm glad, but I want her home." My voice caught on the last word.

His hands settled on my back and patted me. "I hear you." He let me go.

Mind on the pages under my bed, I stepped back. "You find a lawyer for her?"

"We did. She'll start working with your mom as soon as they take the tube out. Jaimie can't really communicate much until then." He didn't wait to see how I took this news, but went over to the fridge and took out a cold Dr. Pepper. He popped the top and then pulled out his phone, thumb scrolling.

I sighed. Sometimes nothing changed.

"Kilby's mom was talking to Mom the other day and she mentioned two sets of books."

Dad looked up at me over his phone. Guess some things were more important than e-mail.

"The fire marshal said your mom's computer was destroyed," Dad said. "Lucky for us, Jaimie kept a backup copy here at the house."

Yup, and they were still where I had hidden them.

Dad frowned. "Nancy Everett says she's got copies of ymour Mom's bookkeeping pages that show your mom is guilty."

I looked away. Not anymore. They were deep in Chester's belly, right next to Mom's pages, instead of out where anyone could find them.

Too dangerous to tell Dad about that. Being a lawyer, he might have to give them to the fire marshall. Better to wait until Mom came home or until I knew more about them.

CHAPTER SIXTEEN

Monday is my least favorite day of the week. On top of having to go back to school, I had to figure out what the pages I'd found meant. I'd been up most of the night trying to figure out why they told such different stories. I'd been up all night looking at the pages. I thought that the ones from Mom's purse showed that *she'd* found the problem and taken it to Mr. Nelson. The others showed that *Mrs. Everett* had found the problem and that Mom was the one stealing. The paper rasped against my palms. How was I supposed to know which were the "real books" and which were the fakes?

I was still mad at Dad for not taking me to the hospital the day before, but he had promised to take me after school. Picking up a couple of sheets from both piles, I folded them and laid them on the bed next to my backpack. The rest I took back into my secret room and tucked them safely inside Chester's belly. Secret door closed securely behind me, I grabbed the folded pages in one hand and put them in my science book and slid that in my backpack.

I tripped over Misty in the doorway to the kitchen. Dad looked up and wiggled the hand not holding the phone to one ear. Work. As usual. I kept an eye on him while I dug into the pantry and came up with a couple of blueberry oat bars. I ripped one open and took a bite.

I fingered the flap on my backpack for a minute as I waited for Dad to finish his call. The alarm on my phone rang. Bus time. I looked on the counter for my lunch. No lunch. I resisted slapping my forehead. Of course not, Mom was still in the hospital and Dad wasn't into our routine anymore. I reached over and opened the top of the cookie jar and pulled out some from Mom's emergency cash stash.

I lifted my backpack and pulled out the pages.

"Dad?" I said. He still wasn't off the phone, but I only had a couple of minutes to tell him about the pages and still catch the bus.

He frowned at me and made a slashing motion with one hand.

Nothing had changed. Work was king. Mom and I? We were distractions.

I stuffed the pages back in my pack and shouldered it. I'd give them to Kilby to give to her mother. She was smart too.

I didn't bother waving goodbye. The screen door slapped closed about the time I hit the ground at the base of the front porch steps.

On the bus, I brushed granola bar crumbs off my lap onto the floor. Bitterness ate at me. Dad needed to do better at getting Mom found not guilty than he did in paying attention to me. I had back-up, though. Kilby's mom would be able to help once my friend got these pages to her.

I hadn't heard a thing my teachers said during my morning classes. As I went through the lunch line, I knew how Justine and Kilby felt. The best choice I could find was a soggy tuna salad sandwich and the usual stale chips and mushy apple. I joined Kilby at our usual lunch table and looked around for Justine and Yasmine. They sat a couple of tables away, carefully not looking our way. Tanner was with them. He kind of waved, but Yasmine smacked his hand down. Ingrid stopped by the table on her way in. Looking my way, she put one hand over her heart to mime a fake, "I am so surprised." Kilby saw her, but neither one of us said anything.

I reached inside my backpack and found my math book. I tugged the ledger pages out and pushed them across the table to Kilby. "What do you think?" I asked.

"I knew there were a lot of riders around, but this is big business." Kilby pointed at the number of the bottom right corner of the page.

"They don't sell a thousand pairs of extra small children's breeches ever, much less in one year," I said. "Why would they order so many?"

"What are those?"

Ingrid. Why couldn't she just leave me alone? She shoved me to one side and grabbed at the papers. Kilby pulled all but the top one away from Ingrid and stuffed them in her backpack. She stuffed the backpack under the lunch table so Ingrid couldn't snatch it too.

Ingrid held the page up. "This doesn't look like homework to me," she said."What did you do with this merchandise?" She read the notation on the side of the page out loud.

Tanner's head swiveled our way. I got up and tried to get the paper back from Ingrid.

"Oh no you don't," Ingrid pulled the paper in to her belly and twisted to the side so I couldn't reach it. For the first time I was sorry she'd made the basketball team. Clearly she was learning defense.

Tanner came up and Ingrid handed him the papers. "Thought you might like to have this."

Tanner looked at it, then frowned at me. "My mom had some just like these," Tanner said. "She showed them to Uncle Ron and Aunt Karen and said they proved your mom stole from them."

I felt like all the air in the room had been sucked away. Then I managed to speak. "Tanner, give that back."

"Mom said—" Tanner began.

"I don't want to hear what your mom said," I interrupted. "We all know what she thinks. She's wrong."

Tanner narrowed his eyes. "Where did you get these? Mom had them. Wait. You stole her purse?"

I opened my mouth to deny it. The lie wouldn't come.

Ingrid started laughing. She walked away.

Tanner glared at me, then turned and headed for the hall.

Kilby looked across the table at me, then over at where Yasmine and Justine sat gawking.

I grabbed my bag and hurried after Tanner.

The bell rang. The last period of the day was finally over. I rose with the rest of the class and shoved my way through the crowded hallway. I hadn't caught up with Tanner. He still had the page, and on top of that, I'd gotten in trouble for being late to class. Just one quick stop at my locker to switch books and I would make him see reason. I fiddled with the lock and yanked the door open. I dropped my backpack on the floor and juggled the packed contents of the locker until I had the stuff I needed for homework.

I picked up a few stray papers and tossed them on top of the stack of books. My shoulder against the steel door convinced it to latch. Ingrid gave me a smirk as I passed her as if she weren't there. She wanted to be the center of attention, so I'd treat her like she was invisible. Getting back at her for real would have to wait. For now this would have to do.

I headed to the auditorium-side of the school. Once there, I scanned the crowd for Tanner. He wasn't there yet.

I leaned against the building. A crowd of kids came out and scattered to wait for their rides.

A minute later Tanner pushed the door open and strolled out.

"You have something you want to give me?" I asked. Unlike earlier, when I was so mad I couldn't see straight, I'd had three hours to think. I started my new mantra.

Be calm.

"I can't." He turned to face me.

"Do you want my mom to go to jail for something she didn't do?" My fingers curled into fists.

I took a deep breath and relaxed my hands.

Stay calm.

Tanner missed my effort because he was concentrating on his toes. "Mom said I had to give it to her."

Another deep breath to keep from screaming.

I took a step toward Tanner. "Hand it over."

He backed up.

I shook my hands out again so that I didn't look like I wanted to hit him, even if I did.

"Seriously, Tanner. Mom's got evidence, too."

Tanner raised a hand. "My mother picked it up an hour ago and took it to the fire marshal."

My fingers clenched at my sides.

Yasmine came out of the building. She hesitated when she saw the two of us together.

A car honked behind me. Yasmine headed for the curb. Mrs. Sengupta had arrived. I stayed put. Queenie took Monday off, so it wasn't a car pool day.

My friend got in the car and it pulled away. As far as I could tell, Yasmine didn't look back at all. When I turned back to Tanner, he was gone too. I slumped against the warm brick of the building outside the gym, wishing I was invisible. The sick feeling wouldn't leave me. I'd come out here to convince Tanner that Mom was innocent and to give back the evidence. But he was right. That paper looked a lot like evidence that Mom had been stealing.

Dad pulled up in Mom's car. I pushed off the wall and went over to get in. As soon as my seat belt clicked, Dad took off.

The mailboxes zipped by on the side of the road.

"You're quiet," Dad said.

I turned to look out the window so he wouldn't see my face.

He shifted in his seat and reached out to put one hand over mine.

"I know this whole thing is hard," he began.

He had no idea.

Dad's phone rang.

I yanked my hand away. Now he'd answer, and leave me to deal with this all on my own. Again.

"Can you hit silent on this thing for me?" Dad asked.

Surprised, I reached out and took the ringing phone from him. "What if it's work?" I asked.

"Not important right now. You're upset. I'm here. Tell me."

Tears pricked my eyes. "I found something this morning," I began. The whole sorry story tumbled out.

I was glad that Dad didn't yell at me for not telling him earlier about Mrs. Everett's purse and the evidence she'd had inside. That might have been because I was crying again by the time I got to the end. He did get very quiet when I told him that Tanner had stolen one of the pages back and given it to his mom and that she'd already given it to the fire marshal.

"Second thing we need to do is talk to your mom about the accounting sheets," Dad said.

"First thing?" I asked.

"Look at the ones we have left and see how they can help your mother."

I blew my nose for the four-thousandth time. Thank goodness Mom saved every spare fast-food napkin that ever entered her car. The glove box was full of them. I splashed some water from my water bottle on my face.

Dad's phone rang again. This time he answered it. "Hey, Charlie," he said. "Okay. Good deal, thanks."

He turned to me. "Uncle Charlie's going to stay with your mom so you and I can have some time together."

For some reason that made me cry even harder.

CHAPTER SEVENTEEN

Clouds blocked most of the afternoon sunshine when Dad pulled in the driveway and around to the back. I climbed out of the car.

Misty was in the yard, going nuts and barking.

"How'd she get out?" Dad asked. "Did you teach this dog to open doors? Could have sworn I left her in the kitchen."

Inside the back gate, I ran up the steps to open the porch door. Dad followed. Misty dashed past me, nearly knocking me down in her eagerness to get inside.

Dad bumped into me when I paused.

"What is it?" he asked.

"That's weird. The back door to the house is open," I said.

Misty dashed inside. A bang sounded, like something heavy hitting the floor, or a door slamming.

Dad shoved the car keys at me. "Go back to the car. Lock yourself inside. Now!"

He didn't look to see if I minded him, but ran into the house.

I hotfooted it around the side of the house to the front.

Misty barked her head off as a silver dually truck sprayed gravel as it sped away. A flash of blond hair under a green baseball cap and a pale oval as the driver looked back were all I saw before Dad burst through the front door. Mr. Nelson had a truck like that. What was he doing in our house? The dog barked again and looked like she was going after the truck. I pounced on Misty before she could get away.

Misty calmed down once the truck was gone. I let her go. She flopped on the ground at my feet waiting for a tummy scratch.

"Did you get a look at them?" Dad asked.

"I think it was Mr. Nelson," I said.

Dad glared down the street where the truck had disappeared. Phone out, Dad called the police. He gave them our address and told them that he thought the guy had gotten away.

"Thanks," he said finally, and ended the call.

Turning to me, he asked, "Where were the papers?"

"My room," I said.

Dad looked from me to the house and back again.

"We're going to go in. I think our intruder is gone, but if I tell you to go lock yourself in the car, you do it. No more ignoring me, young lady. Understand?"

I nodded. This time I would do what he said.

Misty and I followed Dad up the front steps. I stopped in the doorway.

The front door opened into Mom's office. It was trashed. Desk drawers were dumped on the floor, chair shoved against the far wall. Misty nosed at the papers and office supplies piled in the middle of the floor. Even the couch cushions had been torn open. While there wasn't any smoke here, my chest felt like it had in the burning barn.

"Sophie?" Dad said.

I reached out for him, but couldn't see him through my tears. He caught me in a big hug. Breathing got easier once Dad held me. After I filled my lungs a few times, I pulled away.

"Why did they do this?" I asked.

"They were probably after those papers you hid. Do you want to stay here while I go upstairs and check on them?"

"No!" I shook my head hard. "Don't leave me alone!"

One more big breath, then Dad and I picked our way through the mess and headed up to my room.

It took a hand on the doorframe to steady me when I saw my room. The hard band around my chest was back, tighter than ever. My dresser drawers were upended. All those clean clothes I'd washed and put away like Mom liked them after the police had searched my room? Scattered across the floor. One of my Breyer horses lay broken on top of the jumble of clothing. My stomach lurched. I'd never fix it.

I reached for the horse, while Dad pushed a pile of my books from the closet floor into my room. The monster-bell tinkled.

A click, and light spilled out of the closet.

"It's a good thing you were so scared of those monsters in your closet." Dad's voice was muffled. "He didn't get in here."

I followed Dad into the crawl space.

"Where are the papers?" Dad asked.

Kneeling by the rocking horse, I reached inside. The sheets rustled as I put them into Dad's hands.

He held them in the cradle of one arm. Flipping through, he paused a couple of times to read.

He pulled his phone out.

"I'd like to speak to Deborah Saums please." He paused. "Tell the fire marshal it's about the arson at Nelson's Tack Shop."

His voice faded as he moved out into the hall. I crawled over to where I'd hidden my diaries and Luis's lighter. The floorboard was in place. I scooted back and stood, then went back out into the closet and closed the crawl space door. I bent down and picked up *The Girl Who Remembered Horses*. The paperback's spine was ripped halfway through.

I gasped, unable to breathe in before my chest collapsed, all the air whooshing out. It felt like I had one of Mom's cyclones inside me. I sank to the floor. I wanted to go over to the Nelsons' and whip them with the fury that whirled around inside me. This book had gotten me through some tough times during the divorce.

Finally, after about a year—or maybe only a minute—there were no more tears, just the tight ball of anger deep inside my heart. I sucked air into my stiff lungs and shuddered. They could try and mess up my life, but I wasn't going to let them.

I smoothed *Girl's* cover and put it back on the shelf. I bent down and picked up the next book, and the next, and put each book on the shelf in correct order. I held the torn book to my chest when Dad came back in.

"Don't touch those!" he said.

I started to protest. So much in my life was broken right then, surely he could let me put my books back on the shelf.

His next words silenced me.

"The police have to have proof of the break in," he said. "If we clean it all up before they get here, they won't have anything to investigate."

I stepped back. I looked down and felt...empty. Even the anger had deserted me.

"Hold onto that one if you need to," Dad said.

We went down to the kitchen. I didn't know why, but it wasn't as trashed as the rest of the house. Dad called Mom's lawyer to fill him in while we waited for the police to arrive.

"Don't you need to check for fingerprints?" I asked. Everybody knew fingerprints would prove Mr. Nelson had broken into our house.

The policeman looked at me. I could tell he wanted to roll his eyes. "You watch too much television," he said. "We don't usually dust for every break-in, especially when there isn't anything missing."

"This happened right after the fire marshal arrested my ex-wife. Considering Janey is innocent, and she had evidence here at the house that would exonerate her, do you think, Officer, that those two things might be related?" Dad's voice was tight.

I looked down at Dad's hands. My habit of balling my fists was inherited.

"I'll come back if I need to." The policeman clearly didn't think he would ever need to.

I would have slammed the door behind the officer, but Dad pressed it shut carefully.

Once again he pulled out his phone.

"Gail?" he said. Explaining the idiot policeman to Mom's lawyer didn't take long. Gail's tinny voice told Dad that she'd call the police department and light a fire under someone she knew.

Dad slipped his phone back in his pocket.

"Let's get some supper." He turned and headed down the hall.

I skirted the mess in Mom's office and followed him to the kitchen. Dad pulled out the iron skillet and asked me to get out the bread. He pulled cheese and butter from the fridge and proceeded to fix grilled cheese sandwiches.

Normally this kind of dinner would be lip-smacking good, but right then it was going to take a whole lot more than comfort food to make things better. Even though the ingredients were all the same, the sandwich tasted like sawdust. I tried a second bite, but it was just as sad as the first.

"Can I go clean my room now?" I finally asked.

"If the police do come back, they can get prints from your Mom's office."

Dad looked at my plate. His was already bare. He reached over and raised his eyebrows.

"Go ahead," I said.

He bit into the sandwich and in a few bites finished it. From the frown lines above his eyes, I could tell the comfort food hadn't helped him any more than it had me.

Dad put his hands on the table and stood. "You okay up there alone?

At my nod he picked up the plates and took them to the sink.

Misty and I went upstairs. Usually I like my room messy. Even though Mom hates it, I know where everything is.

That night, I didn't know what I would find when I picked things up off the floor. When I wiped my hands down the side of my jeans for the fourteenth time to get the "ick" feeling off from touching things that the intruder had messed up, I decided to take a break. I went out and sat on the top step so I didn't have to look at my room and tried to call Yasmine.

"Leave a message!" her warm voice urged me.

I didn't bother.

My body folded forward on my lap like a broken doll. I was so tired. Too tired to even cry anymore. I closed my eyes and sat there for a long time. The clatter of my phone slipping out of my hand onto the wooden stair tread brought me out of it.

Standing up woke pins and needles in my feet. I hobbled back into my room.

I felt a little better when I tossed the last piece of clothing from the floor into my laundry basket. I hefted it and went downstairs

"You going to clean all of that?" Dad asked when I came through the kitchen.

"I'm not wearing anything until I've washed it all," I said.

"Fair enough," Dad said.

"You want some good news?"

"What?" I asked. What Dad thought of as good news and what I thought was good news were sometimes two different things.

"That last call was your Mom. Charlie's bringing her home."

CHAPTER EIGHTEEN

I hit Mom with a gigantic hug before she could even walk through the front door. Her shirt carried a stale smell that must have come from the hospital. I tensed. She smelled wrong. Then I hugged her even harder. Mom was home. That was all that mattered.

Arms locked around me, Mom pressed her cheek against the top of my head. Misty nearly knocked us both down when she jumped up on Mom. Dad caught the dog's collar and pulled her away before Misty could rip Mom's bandages.

"What the...?" Uncle Charlie's voice broke the mood.

Mom pulled away. She followed Uncle Charlie inside and gasped when she saw the mess in the front room.

"What happened?" She reached down and moved a broken piece of her printer from the top of a pile of papers.

"It was Mr. Nelson." I stared at her to see how she took this news.

Mom glanced at Dad. One eyebrow quirked up.

He nodded. "Sophie is certain it was Nelson's dually we saw drive away."

"It might have been his truck, but it wasn't Ron Nelson who did this." Mom dropped to her knees. She rustled through the papers on the floor. "Nancy Everett drives that truck all the time. I'll bet it was her."

How could she sound so certain? She hadn't seen the truck. Dad gave me the palm-down gesture that said, "Lay off that topic for awhile."

Mom's hands shook when they found her work bag empty. She began to search through the stack of ripped papers in front of her.

I dropped down in a crouch beside her. "Your accounting sheets aren't there. I hid them."

Mom rocked back and stared at me. "You did what?"

Dad spoke up. "Sophie found the pages you brought home from the store. She didn't know if they would help you or make things worse so she hid them."

Mom jumped like she'd forgotten he was there.

Dad started laughing. "I know you said that secret room was a crackpot idea when I built it. But since our burglar didn't find it, you've got to admit it's turned out to be remarkably useful. Just what every child needs is a place to store her mother's alibi, right?"

Mom started toward the stairs. I reached out and grabbed her hand. "We brought them down already." I tugged Mom into the kitchen.

Once there, she sat in front of the stack of papers Dad had put on the table.

The trashed house made me too fidgety to sit. Even though I could see Mom right in front of me, I needed to touch her. I stood behind her and put my hands on her shoulders. Mom's warmth felt wonderful.

She sorted through the pages. Some pages she gripped for a moment, but most of them she discarded as fast as she could pick them up.

"So the officer who came out when you chased off..." Mom said.

"Mr. Nelson. Mom, really." Why wouldn't she believe me?

"Lots of people from the shop use that truck." Mom swallowed hard. "The fire marshal will be here any minute. Where is that stupid signature?" Her hands moved fast as she flipped through the stack.

"There was a truck that started up right after I heard funny noises out in the garage too. I bet Mr. Nelson stole our gas can then, and used it to set his own barn on fire!"

She just gave me a "be quiet" look.

I had told Uncle Charlie about the trashcans before, but I hadn't told anyone about the pages I'd taken to school. Pulling my hands off Mom's shoulders, I folded them across my chest so she wouldn't feel me shake. Why hadn't I kept all the accounting sheets safely hidden in my rocking horse? Tanner took the sheet he stole to his mother. Mr. Nelson was Mrs. Everett's brother. She had to have told him.

I slipped into the empty seat at the table next to Mom. I practiced saying the words in my head, "Mr. Nelson wrecked our house because of me."

I opened my mouth. Nothing came out.

I couldn't tell her, I just couldn't. Scrambling, my brain came up with a thought—surely the pages I'd taken to school weren't the only evidence. I'd tell her later.

Mom turned to me. "Are you sure it was a man driving?"

I jumped a little, and closed my eyes, pretending to think so that she couldn't see how guilty I felt. "All I saw was somebody driving away wearing a green Nelson's Tack baseball cap."

I gathered up my courage and opened my eyes.

Dad and Mom exchanged glances, paying no attention to me.

"Try again," Dad said to Mom. "Some of the pages are stuck together." He reached out and separated a couple of sheets halfway through the stack.

Mom cried, "There it is! The copy of a check I printed out from the bank." She waved the paper at us. "This is for merchandise we never ordered or received. I don't understand what these are though," she said, pointing to the stack she'd made of the sheets I'd taken out of Mrs. Everett's purse.

Dad reached out and took the page Mom said was proof she was innocent.

Proof! Mom was safe. The person who had really done this would go to jail instead of Mom! I didn't have to move to California and leave my friends. A rush of happiness filled me.

"Sophie?" Mom said. "Where did these come from?"

I raised my head. "They were in Mrs. Everett's purse."

Dad's eyes narrowed. "What were you doing snooping in her purse?"

Mom laid a hand on his arm. He pressed his lips together and pulled his arm away. I could tell he was mad, but he didn't say anything else.

"Well, it's a long story," I began.

"Leave her be," Mom said. She ruffled through the pages. "Now I know where those crazy questions the fire marshal asked me came from. And I can show her the real accounting figures from these." She placed a hand on the stack I'd taken from her work bag. "Ron will back me up, since I kept him in the loop for all the questions I had about Nancy's ordering."

Ron. Mr Nelson knew about the money trouble and Mom's questions about Mrs. Everett's ordering? I thought back to all those tiny riding breeches I'd seen the order for. Mrs. Everett was stealing from her own store?

Then I thought about Tanner and how different he'd been lately. He'd been going through everything I was. My heart hardened. Mrs. Everett had hurt Mom, burned down the Nelsons' barn with the ponies still inside. She deserved to go to jail for life.

I ducked out to the hall. I had to tell someone. I pulled out my phone.

I couldn't tell Yasmine her crush's mother was the one who'd burned down both the tack shop and her own brother's barn.

The phone slid back into my pocket as I sat down on the bottom step.

Dad came out. "You need to keep quiet about this for now." He scratched the eyebrow above his right eye while he watched me. He looked right at my phone when he said, "Even Yasmine can't know."

The front doorbell rang. Mom came out of the kitchen and through the hallway to answer the door. It was Deborah Saums, the fire marshal. Dad followed Mom into the living room.

I stayed where I was. I had a lot of thinking to do while the grown-ups talked.

After a little bit, Mom called me in and the fire marshal asked me a bunch of questions. *Yes, I was sure it was the Nelson truck. No, I hadn't seen the person's face.* Then, because Ms. Saums was so nice and understanding, I blurted out about the pages I'd taken to school to show Kilby. When I got to the part about how Ingrid had stolen them and given them to Tanner, it got pretty quiet in the room.

"I did get a delivery today from Mrs. Everett," Ms. Saums said. "But I can see there is another side to this story."

The fire marshal turned to me. "I understand that your mom threatened to turn you in to me because your room was pretty messy."

My eyes opened until I was pretty sure I looked like Cricket did the time the deer crashed out of the bushes right on top of us.

I wasn't sure if she was joking or not, but Mom smiled, so I tried to relax.

"Well, you've got a lifetime pass from getting in trouble for having a messy room."

I started to smile.

But then Ms. Saums added, "But don't ever withhold evidence again. If I'd had these sooner I would have arrested the right person already."

I looked at Mom.

It had taken me hours to get all my clothes clean again. I plucked the last T-shirt out of the laundry basket, folded it, and put it in the drawer Mom insisted should house my shirts.

Uncle Charlie had come over and helped Dad and Mom get some of the living room put back together again. They left around ten. I'd asked Dad to stay, but he said he'd better sleep over at Uncle Charlie's now that Mom was home. Both Mom and Dad seemed to think that with us home the intruder wouldn't dare come back.

I put some of my T-shirts in my drawer. Mom was safe. So why did I want to smash something? I'd collected all of my Pony Pal books and stacked them on top of my dresser. I took both hands and swiped them all onto the floor. A few days before I'd decided to give these to the twins. Would they want them now that I'd helped put their aunt in jail?

Mom's footsteps sounded on the stairs.

My door opened.

Mom tugged me over to the bed and sat down next to me, one arm snug around my shoulders.

Hugs are good. Especially hugs from a Mom you know is going to be around.

"I know it is still tough, honey," she said. "Don't get yourself all worked up about this."

"But, Mom, Mrs. Everett...Tanner..."

"Hush," Mom's voice was stern above my head. "You just hang in there. This should all be resolved in the next day or so."

I pulled away and looked up at her face.

"You heard back from the fire marshal didn't you?"

"Ms. Saums called with some follow-up questions. With the pages we gave her and the search warrant for the shop's account at the bank, I'm pretty sure that she'll have all the proof we need. You really helped, kept me out of jail actually. So... *Go, you!*"

My head dropped against Mom's shoulder. Mom stroked my back, trying to ease the strain away.

"You know what?" I said. "Thinking about someone I know going to jail isn't as bad as you going to jail, but it still stinks."

Mom's face twisted. "Yeah," she said. "It sure does."

After a little while, she went down the hall to her room and I climbed into bed. Laying there in the dark, Misty's warm body snuggled against me, I texted Yasmine. Even if we weren't going to be best friends anymore, I should tell her and Tanner's mom before she heard it from somebody else.

A moment later a text came back. "Can't talk now. See you tomorrow."

Guess that would have to do.

CHAPTER NINETEEN

School did not go well the next day. For one thing, Yasmine wasn't there. Tanner wasn't either. Ingrid smirked at me in the hall after lunch. I ignored her, turning my back to check my phone for messages from Yasmine.

She'd said she'd get back to me. She hadn't.

I worried about what this meant all through the afternoon. At least none of my teachers gave us a pop quiz. I would have hands-down flunked.

Dad picked me up from school. Did he ask me how my day went? Nope. First thing he asked me? "You didn't tell anyone, did you?"

"No." I'd told him I wouldn't and I'd kept that promise, even thought I hated not telling my friends. He missed the glare I shot him. Turned out that Dad noticed my moods almost as much as Yasmine's mom did when we sat in her back seat. That is, not at all. That made me even grumpier.

"You're going the wrong way," I said. "Mom's waiting for us at home." He'd taken the turn toward the stable instead of heading home.

"Nope." Dad took his eyes off the road long enough to glance at me. He shifted the car into higher gear and stepped on the gas. Eyes back on the road, he said, "I talked to Queenie."

"Why?"

"As of today, you're full-leasing the horse." Dad hit the turn signal. He slowed to make the turn into the farm driveway.

Joy ricocheted through me.

"How?" I stammered.

"I didn't realize how important riding was to you before now. I still thought of it as a hobby. After I talked to Queenie, I see now that riding is a serious sport. Worth me taking some extra work so you can ride more often."

He pulled into a parking space and I leaned over to give him a huge hug.

After a minute of that, I was itching to go inside and see *my* horse.

Dad held on to my arm. "Remember what you promised this morning?"

"What?"

He raised his eyebrows. "Don't say anything—not one word," Dad warned.

When I didn't agree right away, he said, "Promise?"

I didn't want to, but he didn't look like he'd let go until I did. "Okay."

Cricket's welcome dance seemed more joyful than usual when I got to her stall. She must know she was mine—all mine. I got even happier when I found that my hand with the new dressing I'd put on it fit inside my riding gloves. If I needed to, I could ride one-handed, but steering the horse was easier with two reins.

Tacked up, I led the mare out to the arena.

My spirits hit the dirt when I passed one of Mrs. Everett's buddies. She said something about "that kid's mother," as I got close to them. The promise Dad had dragged out of me lay like dust in my mouth. I wanted so badly to tell them they were friends with a criminal. Well, he hadn't said anything about dirty looks, so I turned around and stuck my tongue out at them. They started whispering again as soon as I was past them.

Cricket nudged my back as I stood there as if to say, "Never mind them, you're my girl and we need to get riding!"

I straightened my spine and marched out to the arena. *They'd know the truth soon enough.*

Dad sat sideways at the end of the white plastic picnic table, a file folder propped on his lap. A pink dogwood in full bloom provided some shade. He saw me and waved.

It was so Dad. Working. Then I remembered he said he'd be taking on extra work to pay for my horse. Somehow work didn't seem like a dirty word anymore.

Flipping the reins over Cricket's head, I grabbed them in one hand and flung myself on the mare's broad back. She started off pretty crooked, so I urged her to try a relaxed walk. After half a loop around the arena we graduated to serpentines. The half circles, connected with a change of direction in the middle, formed an "S" shape. The exercise was supposed to help Cricket loosen up, and it was especially good because we could bend both to the left and to the right.

Unfortunately, thoughts of Yasmine and her broken promise to call me kept getting in the way of our ride. I shook my head, trying to focus. The fact that I couldn't keep my thoughts where they belonged made me more and more frustrated.

Cricket got stiffer and stiffer as my inner frustration mounted.

It didn't help when I saw Yasmine leading Bourbon into the arena. If she hadn't been at school, how did she get to come to the barn?

I turned Cricket and headed away from her. If she couldn't bother replying to me when I'd told her it was important, then I didn't need to talk to her at all.

I looked over at Dad and found him talking with Mrs. Nelson. Brigette and Brandon sat next to her on the bench.

Cricket felt me tense up. Her tail cranked in the propeller circle she did when she was really annoyed.

"Sorry, girl," I said.

The twins saw me and tore over to greet me.

No way I could face them knowing what I knew about their aunt. I hauled on the left rein and turned Cricket across to the opposite side of the arena. Brigitte's expression crumpled as I headed away. Brandon stopped short and grabbed his sister's arm.

At the opposite rail, I stopped and pretended to adjust my stirrup. Queenie came into the arena with a new student on Tweedle Dee, one of the pair of Shetland lesson ponies she used for beginner riders. The trainer began the lesson, telling the little girl to guide Tweedle Dee out on a circle.

Yasmine pulled Bourbon up at the rail and spoke to the twins like nothing was wrong. I turned away, back stiff. Cricket gave a crow-hop, something she never did.

"Sophie!" Queenie called me over.

I sucked in a breath and managed to get my mare to go in a semi-straight line to the middle of the arena. As soon as I got there, the trainer said, "I have a favor to ask of you."

She called across the arena, "Yasmine, come here."

Yasmine looked at me, and didn't move. She was still mad. Forget this. I was leaving. I kicked Cricket back toward the gate.

"Stop right there," Queenie commanded me.

I sat up straight. Cricket halted.

The trainer came around and ran her hand down Cricket's tense neck. "Get that horse over here," Queenie called to Yasmine. She didn't sound mad, but there was no arguing with Queenie when she said something twice. Yasmine and Bourbon walked toward us.

"Sophie's dad wants to see the *pas de deux* you two did on Dweedle Dum and Tweedle Dee at Yasmine's first Pony Club Rally," Queenie said when we'd arrived. "Think you still remember it?"

As if on cue, I heard the music to The Sorcerer's Apprentice from Disney's *Fantasia* start up at the far rail. I looked over and Dad waved his phone at me. *What was he doing?*

"I don't think..." I gulped as my voice disappeared.

"Don't think. Ride." Queenie's tone was gentle, but her meaning was clear.

I glanced at Yasmine and saw that she'd come to the same conclusion. Best to get going.

We both rode to the gate and turned to face where the judge's stand would be if we were doing this as a competition.

"Start the music again," Queenie called.

As the song began, I squeezed my legs to cue Cricket to pick up a working trot. Yasmine cued Bourbon to do the same. We rode side by side to the center of the arena and halted. We both dropped our right hands in the opening salute.

We rode down the centerline of the arena, Bourbon turning left, Cricket to the right as the music swelled. Now that we'd started, it was easier than I'd thought to ride together. It wasn't like we had to talk to each other. I steered my mare through the next few movements, watching out of the corner of my eye to see if Yasmine and Bourbon were still in sync. They were. While this was the first time Cricket and Bourbon had done this, the two of us girls had practiced this four hundred and twenty times on the ponies the year we did this for competition. It had been so much fun.

The horses picked up the trot again. This routine was so cool. We were good together, Cricket and Bourbon and Yasmine and me. My mouth twitched in a smile as I passed Yasmine on our reverse serpentine loops. Her eyes met mine and I saw an answering smile.

Queenie and the little rider stood to one side, so I had to side-pass to go around them. The trainer leaned over to answer when the little girl asked, "How did she do that?" as Cricket moved away from the wall and then smoothly back again.

The twins came over and climbed up on the fence to flank the trainer. Their grins broadened each time one of us turned their direction. I couldn't help it, I grinned back. For a moment we were all just horse kids together. Cricket and Bourbon passed in front of our imaginary judge, then circled around to halt at the center of the arena as the music ended.

Yasmine and I saluted. I looked over at her.

I had to ask. "Are we going to be okay?"

She nodded. "I hope so."

I took a deep breath. As oxygen filled my lungs, I felt lighter than I had since Yasmine came out of the barn.

Queenie joined us.

The twins jumped down from the fence and ran over to us, boots churning in the dry sandy footing. Brandon reached us first and shouted, "That was great!"

Brigitte arrived next to her brother. "Can you teach us? I bet Star and Raven can do that." Her chestnut curls bounced as she jumped up and down.

Yasmine had been dying to coach the younger ones. "We'd love to," she said.

I looked past the twins. Mrs. Nelson had her phone to her ear. Her face twisted with distress.

Reality crashed my party.

I started to rein Cricket away. Queenie's hand closed over the reins and stopped us cold.

"Stay here," she told me.

Mrs. Nelson called Brandon and Brigitte.

"You'll start showing us Saturday, right?" the twins begged.

Yasmine agreed. Brandon and Brigitte ran to follow their mother as she strode toward the parking lot, phone still stuck to her ear..

Queenie moved away. I guess she figured she'd done her job now that we were talking again.

Yasmine dismounted and turned to me. "I'm sorry I didn't call you last night. I was on the phone with Tanner. His mother...let's just say it was bad. I figured you'd be okay now that your mom is home and cleared."

"You knew?" I couldn't believe it.

"Tanner told me," Yasmine said.

"So why didn't you call today?" I asked.

"I was afraid to," she said. "I thought you hated me for doubting your mom."

"Hate you?" I said. "You're my best friend."

Yasmine's face lit up. "I have so much to tell you," she blurted.

"Me too," I said. "But my dad can't hear us. Let's put the horses up and find someplace to talk."

We remounted and walked our horses around the arena a couple of times. As we made our way to the gate, Cricket seemed happier, moving much more easily than she had when we'd first come into the arena. Not a surprise really, because I sure felt better. I reached down and rubbed her neck. *The Outside of the Horse is Good for the Inside of the Girl,* I told myself, quoting another horsey T-shirt.

Horses and friends. Nothing beat those two things.

CHAPTER TWENTY

Yasmine and I brought our horses into the wash rack. I felt pretty darn good. Yasmine and I were back to being friends. I had a full lease on Cricket. The only thing missing was everyone knowing my mom was innocent. And that would come sooner rather than later. I whistled a tune from the latest Taylor Swift album. She'd been in Pony Club, too, Queenie said sometimes, back when she was little.

Horses clean, I picked up Cricket's wash bucket, unclipped my horse from the cross ties and looked around to make sure I'd gotten everything. Sponge, scraper, shampoo. Check.

"See you in the tack room?" I said to Yasmine.

"Yup. Just have to get his face rinsed off and I'm done."

Once I had Cricket back in her stall, I put a couple of carrots in her feed tub. It might be spring, but it still got kind of cold at night. Rummaging through the grooming kit, I found the rub rag and went to work on her coat to help my horse dry off. That done, I took the saddle and bridle back to the tack room.

Arms free after Cricket's saddle slipped onto its bar, I slipped the bridle off my shoulder and hung it on the hook that had the mare's name on it. I used my rub rag to wipe the slime off the bit.

Now that I had a full lease on my horse, I needed to step up my game. I got the bridle down again. It didn't take a lot of extra time to wind the throat latch in a figure eight. Back in place, it looked pretty good hanging there nice and neat. I turned toward the door and stopped. Tanner stood there, fists shoved in his pockets, gaze darting from side to side, looking at everything but me.

"You gave the fire marshal papers from the wrong set of books," he said.

I scrunched up my nose. Trying to remember that he was my friend took a lot of effort.

"That accounting sheet of your mom's? The one you stole back from me? It was a fake. Your mom was the one stealing from the store. She set those fires and you helped her frame my mother."

"My mom would never—"

"I said that too, remember? But I was right."

Tanner's face flushed. "Mom says —"

If he hadn't helped his mom I could have felt sorry for him. I hardened my heart. "Your mom is lying to you." I turned to pick up my backpack so that I could go home.

When I faced Tanner again, Mrs. Everett stood inside the tack room door. She almost looked normal. Her blonde hair was tied back in her usual sleek ponytail, makeup perfect down to the last detail. But her eyes had a dead look to them that made me shiver.

I slipped my right hand into my bag and found my phone.

She turned to Tanner. "Go wait in the truck for me. I'll straighten her out."

Tanner's face paled, and he backed away.

While her attention on her retreating son, I peeked at the phone and was able to dial my Dad. A tiny "hello?" from my bag let me know I'd gotten through.

"You don't look so good, Mrs. Everett." I hoped my voice was loud enough that Dad could hear me. When Mrs. Everett came toward me, I took a step back. It wasn't like I could go far, since the line of plastic tack trunks under the bridle hooks took up a lot of the room. As she took another step forward, I sat on the lip of the open trunk and reached behind me. My fingers closed on the crop I knew was there.

Mrs. Everett grabbed me.

"Let me go," I hollered.

Mrs. Everett's hand tightened and she twisted my arm, hauling me up onto my feet and jerking me toward the door. "I'm going to —"

I cried out at the burst of pain in my shoulder. I had to get away. I brought the crop up and whipped it down on the arm she used to drag me. The tail of the crop stung against my arm, but I barely felt it. This woman had lost it. A little pain was worth it if I got away.

She let go of my wrist and whirled around. I drew the crop back again, ready to strike again if I needed to.

Mrs. Everett grabbed the crop and ripped it out of my hand. She raised her arm and I scrambled backward. As she began to bring the crop down on me, I tripped on something lying on the floor. My head hit the corner of the trunk and I never felt if the whip connected.

I awoke to blackness. A lump under my shoulder blade dug into my back, so I tried to sit up. My head whacked against a hard surface. I gasped in pain and a sharp antiseptic smell filled my nose, making my eyes water. Reaching out with my hands, I felt smooth plastic to either side, above and below me. The crazy woman had shoved me inside of a tack trunk. I sucked in air, but then couldn't catch my breath from the fumes. Desperate, I shoved my nose toward the seam where the lid met the body of the trunk. There was a trickle of fresher air there but my whole body still felt like screaming. I had to get out. Being trapped in that trunk was making me as scared as being on a runaway horse.

Almost as soon as that thought popped into my head, I knew what to do. Breathe in, two, three, four. Breathe out, two, three, four. Thanks to Queenie's teaching, my head cleared.

From the vibrations, and the muffled sounds I could hear, Mrs. Everett must have thrown the trunk in the back of her truck. I needed to get out of there. If I got the lid open, I could signal that I needed help.

Bringing my knees to my chest, I pushed up. No luck. My hands slid over the plastic, coming to rest when I felt a metal rectangle on the wall to my right. The latch. My nails pried at the edges, but no way to open it from inside.

I felt around me. A lone bandage and that stinky jar of Furisone were all I could find. I guess I took up enough room that Mrs. Everett had dumped everything out before stuffing me inside. I shifted and the lump poked me in the back again. I wiggled just enough to get the object out from under me. A hoof pick. Not a hammer, but it gave me something to work with. I tried to get the tip of the pick under the metal plate, but it was too thick to fit. I tried hitting it, but the pick slid off the metal plate and gouged the plastic next to it. I blinked a couple of times. The spot where I'd scraped the plastic seemed lighter. I dug at the plastic with the hoof pick.

A hole the size of a dime appeared, and then became a quarter-sized slice of light. The vibrations changed. *Had she seen me? Why else would she slow down?*

The hoof pick fell from my fingers as I slid and hit the end of the trunk. We'd turned.

The vibrations picked up again. I ran my fingers around the floor of the trunk and found the pick. My scraping got more frantic as the truck picked up speed. I didn't know where we were going, but if Mrs. Everett would stuff me in a trunk, she might do anything. I wasn't going to be stuck in that trunk when we arrived. A few more frantic moments of gouging the plastic and I could fit a hand out of the opening.

The truck slowed again, and I listened carefully to see if they had seen my hand when I felt for the lock. All I heard was road noise, so I stuck my arm out all the way to the elbow and held my breath. *Please, don't let there be a padlock.*

The smooth feel of a double-ended snap bought my lips back in a fierce smile. I could open one of those in my sleep. Thumbing it open, I dropped it in the bed of the truck. The latch fell open. I pushed the lid open a crack.

The fresh air was wonderful. The truck braked and the trunk lid flew open. Mrs. Everett yelled as she spun the steering wheel. Tanner stared at me out the back window, mouth agape, and tears running down his face.

I shoved myself out of the tack trunk and fell on the truck bed. Mrs. Everett floored the gas. I slid across the bed lining and hit the tailgate. A bunch of stuff came with me and banged into my legs as I grabbed the side to haul myself up. I peered over the side. The truck turned sharply onto a gravel road. No way was I going down a lonely dirt road with this lady. I flipped the latch on the tailgate and pushed it open, then jumped and slid out over the end.

I hit the ground hard, copper taste flooding my mouth. The gravel road was even harder than arena sand. It hurt so much I almost couldn't open my eyes. The truck's engine stopped. I heard a door open. It didn't matter how much I hurt, it was time to move. I rolled over and got up on my hands and knees. Unfortunately, I couldn't get enough breath back to get on my feet.

Tanner flung himself out of the passenger side of the truck and ran after his Mom. He caught up and tried to tackle her from behind. Mrs. Everett shook Tanner off and came toward me. I scrambled back, and one hand closed on a metal rod. It must have fallen out of the back of the truck when I opened the tailgate. Mrs. Everett leaned over me, and I brought it up and hit her as hard as I could. She fell to the ground, took a ragged breath, then started to get up again.

Tanner tackled her, knocking her back to the ground. "Go!" he cried out to me.

I got my feet under me, then stood up and lurched toward the highway.

Sirens sounded off to the left, coming closer. I looked back. Mrs. Everett stopped fighting. Tanner slid off his mom and squatted next to her.

Mrs. Everett reached up and stroked Tanner's hair back from his face. "Baby, you know I'd never hurt anyone," she said.

He drew back just enough that she couldn't reach his face. "Why did you do it, Mom?"

Sitting up, Mrs. Everett tried to reach out again to her son. Once again, he avoided her touch. "I just wanted to buy a decent horse for you."

Mrs. Everett continued, "I stayed home from market because I knew your Uncle Ron was going to find out what I'd done. Then I found a way out. All the evidence pointing to me was right there on Jaimie Allen's desk. I put them in the trashcan and set it on fire. Then I couldn't put it out."

Tanner stood up all the way and took another step toward my side. "You didn't have to burn down Brigette and Brandon's barn with the ponies inside."

Mrs. Everett's head tucked down. Her hand spasmed in the gravel and for a moment I thought she was going to fling it up in our faces. A police car pulled off the highway and skidded to a stop a few feet away.

As the door opened and a policewoman got out, Tanner stared at his mother.

The officer nodded at us. "You both all right?" she asked.

At our nods, the policewoman spread her hands wide and walked slowly toward Mrs. Everett.

"Nancy Everett?" the policewoman asked.

"I never hurt Sophie. She fell and hurt herself," Mrs. Everett said. Her voice sounded like some Sesame Street character, all high and singsongy.

"Put your hands behind your head," The policewoman said.

Mrs. Everett looked at me. Her face twisted with a rage so hot that I took a step back. Tanner backed away with me. Mrs. Everett's expression went blank, eyes unfocused and empty, like she'd walked out of her own body.

The policewoman grabbed Tanner's mom and pulled her arms behind her, closing the handcuffs around Mrs. Everett's wrists. She never once moved.

Mom's car squealed in. Dad leapt out and got to me in two steps. "We found you!" His hands patted me all over as if checking to make sure I was all there.

I threw my arms around him. "I'm fine, really I am."

The passenger door opened. Queenie's voice said, "Tanner, you all right?" I looked up to see her reach out and pull Tanner into a hug. *Safe.* I closed my eyes and turned my head into Dad's shoulder.

CHAPTER TWENTY-ONE

No one had seen Tanner in the week since his mother had been arrested. He hadn't been at school, and the new owner had picked Vee up and trailered him back to her farm. Given how mean everyone had been to me and Mom when Mrs. Everett had everyone thinking Mom had done all the horrible things Mrs. Everett had done, I didn't blame him for not coming around. Yasmine had talked to him a few times. Mrs. Everett was in jail, and my mom was completely cleared. Mr. Nelson was talking to contractors about rebuilding the store, and Dad had flown back to California. I'd promised to spend four weeks with him instead of two the following summer, which would be hard. But it was fair. He loved me too and I needed to be with him more than I had.

Even though Queenie had warned us that today was going to be a big day for all of us, it felt good when I saw Tanner come out of the barn, leading Queenie's best lesson horse, Froggie.

"Jazzy!" I hissed.

Yasmine's head whipped around, and I saw her take a step in his direction. She jerked to a halt as soon as she realized what she had done and turned to fiddle with Bourbon's bridle. "Sorry," she said to me.

"It's okay," I replied.

And it was. When Queenie had told us he'd be coming for the Pony Club meeting that week, Mom and I had sat down and talked for a long time about how I felt about it. As mad as I was about everything he had done, I kept coming back to the fact that he was a friend. And after I'd had time to think hard about it, I figured that he hadn't done anything that I wouldn't have done for my Mom. It would be weird, but we'd figure it out. Besides, Yasmine still liked him.

Queenie strode out to meet Tanner. She placed one hand on his shoulder while she bent her head and spoke to him. He straightened up and looked over in our direction. I quickly looked away, not sure how he was going to react to me. Just because I was willing to still be his friend didn't mean he felt the same way.

Once we all got on and started to ride, Tanner circled so that he was at the opposite end of the arena from Cricket and me. Queenie kept giving patient instruction that would end with Cricket and me right back with Tanner and Froggie. After fifteen minutes of this, Tanner gave up trying to have his lesson at the far end of the arena and rode where the movements took him.

After one particularly nice lengthening across the diagonal, I called out, "Nice job."

Tanner whipped his head around to look at me so quickly he nearly fell off the horse. His eyes were wide, mouth open as he took in a deep breath. My gut muscles tensed. I knew that expression. He'd been afraid. I knew exactly how that felt. I smiled in his direction to show him I wasn't mad anymore, but he'd already turned away.

"Okay," said Queenie. "Think that's enough for today. Yasmine and Sophie, remember you've got a musical practice with the twins later. Take care of your horses like usual, then meet them back here."

Tanner was gone before we could even dismount. I pressed my knuckles down into the soft hair covering Cricket's neck, completely frustrated. I'd even practiced talking to my friend in front of a mirror, and he just left.

I swung my leg over the back of the saddle and slid to the ground. Drawing the reins over Cricket's head, I loosened the girth and ran the stirrups up.

Queenie came up beside me. "You can catch up with him in Froggie's stall," she said. "He wanted to talk to you someplace where a bunch of people weren't watching. Then bring him to the gathering."

My hand stilled on the stirrups, then finished threading the leather back through the iron to keep it run up. I drew Cricket's reins back over her head and led her back toward the barn.

Tanner was in the stall, brushing the heck out of Froggie's tail. I led Cricket into her stall, pulled the tack off of her, and put it carefully on the ground outside her door. Then I walked across the aisle and went into Froggie's stall with Tanner. I picked up a comb out of Tanner's grooming kit and started on Froggie's mane.

"I'm glad you're back," I said.

"I don't know if I should even be here," Tanner said. "People keep whispering."

"They did that to me. It stopped, eventually."

"Only because they had my mom to talk about."

I rested my hand on Froggie's neck and turned to Tanner. "Pretty soon there will be something else to talk about. We know you, Tanner. You're our friend. You always do the right thing. Like when you and I figured out how to save those ponies. And when you helped me with your mom."

Tanner ducked his head. Froggie snorted and nosed him for his treat.

A woman walked by, carefully not looking at the two of us. I gave her a big smile. She frowned a little. Then when she got a few steps farther down the aisle, turned around to walk backwards a few steps, gave me a tiny smile in return, then moved on her way.

Tanner shook his head, picked up the curry and hard brush and started giving the horse a brisk rubdown. I riffled through his brush box, found the hoof pick, and went to work on my side. First the foreleg. Round the outside, back to front on the underneath portion. Drop the hoof and apply oil. Moving to the back, I struggled to convince the horse to pick up his hind, and finally got it up far enough to get that one done. I handed the pick and can of hoof oil to Tanner, accepted the curry and hard brush, and went up to the neck to start the process on my side.

Done in no time at all. We went across the aisle and groomed Cricket together.

As Tanner shut the stall door, he said, "You don't have to hang out with me, you know."

"Tanner, even when it looked like my mom was going to jail, you were still my friend. Besides, Yasmine still has a crush on you."

The shadows in his green eyes lightened a fraction as his lips tugged upward.

"Now," I said, "Will you come with me for a moment?"

"Where?" he said. "Dad's waiting in the parking lot."

"He won't be worried. This is on the way." I led him out the end of the barn and down the hill toward the path to the woods. The kids in the Pony Club stood there. Each one of them came up and put a hand out to either hug Tanner or shake his hand. I don't know about Tanner, but my eyes were moist by the time we all turned and started walking out to the field where Queenie's oak stood. It took awhile. By the time we got there, the bigs kids were carrying little kids in mock horse races. As soon as we got to the oak, everyone swarmed up the tree. The branches soon held about twenty kids.

I left Tanner with Queenie under the tree and climbed up to sit next to Brigitte. She snuggled up against me. Queenie put both hands on Tanner's shoulder and bent down to whisper in his ear. He thought for a moment, then nodded and put his hand up to cup her ear as he whispered back. Then he shook hands with Queenie, and reached up for the first branch. He climbed the tree to where Yasmine sat, blushing. Queenie passed the pocketknife to the lowest child. It went up from hand to hand until it reached him.

He carved his initials. I grinned a little when I noticed that he'd chosen the limb next to Yasmine's so that their initials stood together on the trunk. He didn't add a plus sign, but there was sure room for one if they wanted to add it later. Closing the knife, he stuck it in his pocket and leaned back against the trunk. He looked down at Queenie, and then over at me and Brigitte. Brandon mimed a high five at his cousin. Tanner turned last to Yasmine, who sat on the other side of the trunk from him. I was so glad we had done this as a club. He belonged with us and was always welcome.

That done, we all came back down out of the tree and walked back to the barn. The twins ran ahead, yelling back that they'd see us in the ring. The rest of us kids strolled in small groups, with Queenie, as always, herding us all along.

Discussion Questions

1. Horses are smart, strong, and loving. Working with a horse can make you stronger, more organized, and more responsible. Those things come because horses take a lot of work. Sophie, Yasmine, and Tanner did some of the things needed to take care of their own horses. If you were to buy or lease a horse, do you think you could work hard enough to take care of one?

2. Friends are really important. Do you think Sophie, Yasmine, and Tanner were good friends? Do you think you could stay friends with someone if they had to let you down?

3. I added a boy to Sophie's ride group on purpose. Not as many boys ride these days as girls, but that wasn't always true. Not too long ago, riding or driving horses was the way that people got from one place to another. My grandfather sold shoes along the Blue Ridge Mountains, and drove a matched pair of horses to pull his wagon. Why do you think more girls ride than boys these days?

4. The scene with the fire was very hard for me to write. Many of the things I thought I knew about fires were wrong. Only a trained firefighter should go inside a burning building —it is VERY dangerous. Sophie and Tanner would have been hurt pretty badly if they had tried to save these ponies in real life. How else could Sophie and Tanner have saved Star and Raven without actually going inside the barn?

5. I gave Sophie many of my own favorite books to read. Some of them I love because of the adventure. So often, too, the character becomes a friend once the book is finished. What books do you like to read and why?

6. The ending was something I saw from the beginning. Writing about a parent going to jail for making a really bad choice was hard. How would you feel if you were Sophie and knew that your mom might get in a lot of trouble for something she didn't do?

About the Author

Julie Wray Herman lives on a small organic farm outside Houston, Texas, where she and her ever-patient husband ride herd on the ever-shifting population of the farm. At last count they had two retired quarter horse mares, a cat, and the creature that lurks in the pond. Julie serves as a Chief Horse Management Judge for the United States Pony Clubs and on the board of Writespace, a Houston area writers' treasure trove of resources.

CPSIA information can be obtained
at www.ICGtesting.com
Printed in the USA
LVOW08s2047060617

537124LV00005BA/941/P

9 780997 457537